The Circular Study

Anna Katharine Green

Alpha Editions

ISBN : 9789353291495

Design and Setting By
Alpha Editions
email - alphaedis@gmail.com

Contents

BOOK I

A STRANGE CRIME

CHAPTER I

RED LIGHT

Mr. Gryce was melancholy. He had attained that period in life when the spirits flag and enthusiasm needs a constant spur, and of late there had been a lack of special excitement, and he felt dull and superannuated. He was even contemplating resigning his position on the force and retiring to the little farm he had bought for himself in Westchester; and this in itself did not tend to cheerfulness, for he was one to whom action was a necessity and the exercise of his mental faculties more inspiring than any possible advantage which might accrue to him from their use.

But he was not destined to carry out this impulse yet. For just at the height of his secret dissatisfaction there came a telephone message to Headquarters which roused the old man to something like his former vigor and gave to the close of this gray fall day an interest he had not expected to feel again in this or any other kind of day. It was sent from Carter's well-known drug store, and was to the effect that a lady had just sent a boy in from the street to say that a strange crime had been committed in ———'s mansion round the corner. The boy did not know the lady, and was shy about showing the money she had given him, but that he had money was very evident, also, that he was frightened enough for his story to be true. If the police wished to communicate with him, he could be found at Carter's, where he would be detained till an order for his release should be received.

A *strange* crime! That word "strange" struck Mr. Gryce, and made him forget his years in wondering what it meant. Meanwhile the men about him exchanged remarks upon the house brought thus unexpectedly to their notice. As it was one of the few remaining landmarks of the preceding century, and had been made conspicuous moreover by the shops, club-houses, and restaurants pressing against it on either side, it had been a marked spot for years even to those who knew nothing of its history or traditions.

And now a crime had taken place in it! Mr. Gryce, in whose ears that word "strange" rang with quiet insistence, had but to catch the eye of the inspector in charge to receive an order to investigate the affair. He started at once, and proceeded first to the drug store. There he found the boy, whom he took along with him to the house indicated in the message. On the way he made him talk, but there was nothing the poor waif could add to the story already sent over the telephone. He persisted in saying that a lady (he did not say woman) had come up to him while he was looking at some toys in a window, and, giving him a piece of money, had drawn him along the street as far as the drug store. Here she showed him another coin, promising to add it to the one he had already pocketed if he would run in to the telephone clerk with a message for the police. He wanted the money, and when he grabbed at it she said that all he had to do was to tell the clerk that a strange crime had been committed in the old house on —— Street. This scared him, and he was sliding off, when she caught him again and shook him until his wits came back, after which he ran into the store and delivered the message.

There was candor in the boy's tone, and Mr. Gryce was disposed to believe him; but when he was asked to describe the lady, he showed that his powers of observation were no better than those of most of his class. All he could say was that she was a stunner, and wore shiny clothes and jewels, and Mr. Gryce, recognizing the lad's limitations at the very moment he found himself in view of the house he was making for, ceased to question him, and directed all his attention to the building he was approaching.

Nothing in the exterior bespoke crime or even disturbance. A shut door, a clean stoop, heavily curtained windows (some of which were further shielded by closely drawn shades) were eloquent of inner quiet and domestic respectability, while its calm front of brick, with brownstone trimmings, offered a pleasing contrast to the adjoining buildings jutting out on either side, alive with signs and humming with business.

"Some mistake," muttered Gryce to himself, as the perfect calm reigning over the whole establishment struck him anew. But before he had decided that he had been made the victim of a hoax, a movement took place in the area under the stoop, and an officer stepped out, with a countenance expressive of sufficient perplexity

- 3 -

for Mr. Gryce to motion him back with the hurried inquiry: "Anything wrong? Any blood shed? All seems quiet here."

The officer, recognizing the old detective, touched his hat. "Can't get in," said he. "Have rung all the bells. Would think the house empty if I had not seen something like a stir in one of the windows overhead. Shall I try to make my way into the rear yard through one of the lower windows of Knapp & Co.'s store, next door?"

"Yes, and take this boy with you. Lock him up in some one of their offices, and then break your way into this house by some means. It ought to be easy enough from the back yard."

The officer nodded, took the boy by the arm, and in a trice had disappeared with him into the adjoining store. Mr. Gryce remained in the area, where he was presently besieged by a crowd of passers-by, eager to add their curiosity to the trouble they had so quickly scented. The opening of the door from the inside speedily put an end to importunities for which he had as yet no reply, and he was enabled to slip within, where he found himself in a place of almost absolute quiet. Before him lay a basement hall leading to a kitchen, which, even at that moment, he noticed to be in trimmer condition than is usual where much housework is done, but he saw nothing that bespoke tragedy, or even a break in the ordinary routine of life as observed in houses of like size and pretension.

Satisfied that what he sought was not to be found here, he followed the officer upstairs. As they emerged upon the parlor floor, the latter dropped the following information:

"Mr. Raffner of the firm next door says that the man who lives here is an odd sort of person whom nobody knows; a bookworm, I think they call him. He has occupied the house six months, yet they have never seen any one about the premise but himself and a strange old servant as peculiar and uncommunicative as his master."

"I know," muttered Mr. Gryce. He did know, everybody knew, that this house, once the seat of one of New York's most aristocratic families, was inhabited at present by a Mr. Adams, noted alike for his more than common personal attractions, his wealth, and the uncongenial nature of his temperament, which precluded all association with his kind. It was this knowledge which had given zest to this investigation. To enter the house of such a man was an event in itself: to enter it on an errand of life and death—Well, it is under the inspiration of such opportunities that life is reawakened in old veins, especially when those veins connect the heart and brain of a sagacious, if octogenarian, detective.

The hall in which they now found themselves was wide, old-fashioned, and sparsely furnished in the ancient manner to be observed in such time-honored structures. Two doors led into this hall, both of which now stood open. Taking advantage of this fact, they entered the nearest, which was nearly opposite the top of the staircase they had just ascended, and found themselves in a room barren as a doctor's outer office. There was nothing here worth their attention, and they would have left the place as unceremoniously as they had entered it if they had not caught glimpses of richness which promised an interior of uncommon elegance, behind the half-drawn folds of a portière at the further end of the room.

Advancing through the doorway thus indicated, they took one look about them and stood appalled. Nothing in their experience (and they had both experienced much) had prepared them for the thrilling, the solemn nature of what they were here called upon to contemplate.

Shall I attempt its description?

A room small and of circular shape, hung with strange tapestries relieved here and there by priceless curios, and lit, although it was still daylight, by a jet of rose-colored light concentrated, not on the rows and rows of books around the lower portion of the room, or on the one great picture which at another time might have drawn the eye and held the attention, but on the upturned face of a man lying on a bearskin rug with a dagger in his heart and on his breast a cross whose golden lines, sharply outlined against his long, dark, swathing garment, gave him the appearance of a saint prepared in some holy place for burial, save that the dagger spoke of violent death, and his face of an anguish for which Mr. Gryce, notwithstanding his lifelong experience, found no name, so little did it answer to a sensation of fear, pain, or surprise, or any of the emotions usually visible on the countenances of such as have fallen under the unexpected stroke of an assassin.

CHAPTER II

MYSTERIES

A moment of indecision, of awe even, elapsed before Mr. Gryce recovered himself. The dim light, the awesome silence, the unexpected surroundings recalling a romantic age, the motionless figure of him who so lately had been the master of the house, lying outstretched as for the tomb, with the sacred symbol on his breast offering such violent contradiction to the earthly passion which had driven the dagger home, were enough to move even the tried spirit of this old officer of the law and confuse a mind which, in the years of his long connection with the force, had had many serious problems to work upon, but never one just like this.

It was only for a moment, though. Before the man behind him had given utterance to his own bewilderment and surprise, Mr. Gryce had passed in and taken his stand by the prostrate figure.

That it was that of a man who had long since ceased to breathe he could not for a moment doubt; yet his first act was to make sure of the fact by laying his hand on the pulse and examining the eyes, whose expression of reproach was such that he had to call up all his professional sangfroid to meet them.

He found the body still warm, but dead beyond all question, and, once convinced of this, he forbore to draw the dagger from the wound, though he did not fail to give it the most careful attention before turning his eyes elsewhere. It was no ordinary weapon. It was a curio from some oriental shop. This in itself seemed to point to suicide, but the direction in which the blade had entered the body and the position of the wound were not such as would be looked for in a case of self-murder.

The other clews were few. Though the scene had been one of bloodshed and death, the undoubted result of a sudden and fierce attack, there were no signs of struggle to be found in the well-ordered apartment. Beyond a few rose leaves scattered on the floor, the room was a scene of peace and quiet luxury. Even the large table which occupied the centre of the room and near which the master of the house had been standing when struck gave no token of the tragedy which had been enacted at its side. That is, not at first glance; for though its large top was covered with articles of use and ornament, they all stood undisturbed and presumably in place, as if the shock which had laid their owner low had failed to be communicated to his belongings.

The contents of the table were various. Only a man of complex tastes and attainments could have collected and arranged in one small compass pipes, pens, portraits, weights, measures, Roman lamps, Venetian glass, rare porcelains, medals, rough metal work, manuscript, a scroll of music, a pot of growing flowers, and— and—(this seemed oddest of all) a row of electric buttons, which Mr. Gryce no sooner touched than the light which had been burning redly in the cage of fretted ironwork overhead changed in a twinkling to a greenish glare, filling the room with such ghastly tints that Mr. Gryce sought in haste another button, and, pressing it, was glad to see a mild white radiance take the place of the sickly hue which had added its own horror to the already solemn terrors of the spot.

"Childish tricks for a man of his age and position," ruminated Mr. Gryce; but after catching another glimpse of the face lying upturned at his feet he was conscious of a doubt as to whether the owner of that countenance could have possessed an instinct which was in any wise childish, so strong and purposeful were his sharply cut features. Indeed, the face was one to make an impression under any circumstances. In the present instance, and with such an expression stamped upon it, it exerted a fascination which disturbed the current of the detective's thoughts whenever by any chance he allowed it to get between him and his duty. To attribute folly to a man with such a mouth and such a chin was to own one's self a poor judge of human nature. Therefore, the lamp overhead, with its electric connection and changing slides, had a meaning which at present could be sought for only in the evidences of scientific research observable in the books and apparatus everywhere surrounding him.

Letting the white light burn on, Mr. Gryce, by a characteristic effort, shifted his attention to the walls, covered, as I have said, with tapestries and curios. There was nothing on them calculated to aid him in his research into the secret of this crime, unless—yes, there *was* something, a bent-down nail, wrenched from its place, the nail on which the cross had hung which now lay upon the dead man's heart. The cord by which it had been suspended still clung to the cross and mingled its red threads with that other scarlet thread which had gone to meet it from the victim's wounded breast. Who had torn down that cross? Not the victim himself. With such a wound, any such movement would have been impossible. Besides, the nail and the empty place on the wall were as far removed from where he lay as was possible in the somewhat circumscribed area of this circular apartment. Another's hand, then, had pulled down this symbol of peace and pardon, and placed it where the dying man's fleeting breath would play across it, a peculiar exhibition of religious hope or mad remorse, to the significance of which Mr. Gryce could not devote more than a passing thought, so golden were the moments in which he found himself alone upon this scene of crime.

Behind the table and half-way up the wall was a picture, the only large picture in the room. It was the portrait of a young girl of an extremely interesting and pathetic beauty. From her garb and the arrangement of her hair, it had evidently been painted about the end of our civil war. In it was to be observed the same haunting quality of intellectual charm visible in the man lying prone upon the floor, and though she was fair and he dark, there was sufficient likeness between the two to argue some sort of relationship between them. Below this picture were fastened a sword, a pair of epaulettes, and a medal such as was awarded for valor in the civil war.

"Mementoes which may help us in our task," mused the detective.

Passing on, he came unexpectedly upon a narrow curtain, so dark of hue and so akin in pattern to the draperies on the adjoining walls that it had up to this time escaped his attention. It was not that of a window, for such windows as were to be seen in this unique apartment were high upon the wall, indeed, almost under the ceiling. It must, therefore, drape the opening into still another communicating room. And such he found to be the case. Pushing this curtain aside, he entered a narrow closet containing a bed, a dresser, and a small table. The bed was the narrow cot of a bachelor, and the dresser that of a man of luxurious tastes and the utmost nicety of habit. Both the bed and dresser were in perfect order, save for a silver-backed comb, which had been taken from the latter, and which he presently found lying on the floor at the other end of the room. This and the presence of a pearl-handled parasol on a small stand near the door proclaimed that a woman had been there within a short space of time. The identity of this woman was soon established in his eyes by a small but unmistakable token connecting her with the one who had been the means of sending in the alarm to the police. The token of which I speak was a little black spangle, called by milliners and mantua-makers a sequin, which lay on the threshold separating this room from the study; and as Mr. Gryce, attracted by its sparkle, stooped to examine it, his eye caught sight of a similar one on the floor beyond, and of still another a few steps farther on. The last one lay close to the large centre-table before which he had just been standing.

The dainty trail formed by these bright sparkling drops seemed to affect him oddly. He knew, minute observer that he was, that in the manufacture of this garniture the spangles are strung on a thread which, if once broken, allows them to drop away one by one, till you can almost follow a woman so arrayed by the sequins that fall from her. Perhaps it was the delicate nature of the clew thus offered that pleased him, perhaps it was a recognition of the irony of fate in thus making a trap for unwary mortals out of their vanities. Whatever it was, the smile with which he turned his eye upon the table toward which he had thus been led was very eloquent. But before examining this article of furniture more closely, he attempted to find out where the thread had become loosened which had let the spangles fall. Had it caught on any projection in doorway or furniture? He saw none. All the chairs were cushioned and—But wait! there was the cross! That had a fretwork of gold at its base. Might not this filagree have caught in her dress as she was tearing down the cross from the wall and so have started the thread which had given him this exquisite clew?

Hastening to the spot where the cross had hung, he searched the floor at his feet, but found nothing to confirm his conjecture until he had reached the rug on which the prostrate man lay. There, amid the long hairs of the bearskin, he came upon one other spangle, and knew that the woman in the shiny clothes had stooped there before him.

Satisfied on this point, he returned to the table, and this time subjected it to a thorough and minute examination. That the result was not entirely unsatisfactory was evident from the smile with which he eyed his finger after having drawn it across a certain spot near the inkstand, and also from the care with which he lifted that inkstand and replaced it in precisely the same spot from which he had taken it up. Had he expected to find something concealed under it? Who can tell? A detective's face seldom yields up its secrets.

He was musing quite intently before this table when a quick step behind him made him turn. Styles, the officer, having now been over the house, had returned, and was standing before him in the attitude of one who has something to say.

"What is it?" asked Mr. Gryce, with a quick movement in his direction.

For answer the officer pointed to the staircase visible through the antechamber door.

"Go up!" was indicated by his gesture.

Mr. Gryce demurred, casting a glance around the room, which at that moment interested him so deeply. At this the man showed some excitement, and, breaking silence, said:

"Come! I have lighted on the guilty party. He is in a room upstairs."

"He?" Mr. Gryce was evidently surprised at the pronoun.

"Yes; there can be no doubt about it. When you see him—but what is that? Is he coming down? I'm sure there's nobody else in the house. Don't you hear footsteps, sir?"

Mr. Gryce nodded. Some one was certainly descending the stairs.

"Let us retreat," suggested Styles. "Not because the man is dangerous, but because it is very necessary you should see him before he sees you. He's a very strange-acting man, sir; and if he comes in here, will be sure to do something to incriminate himself. Where can we hide?"

Mr. Gryce remembered the little room he had just left, and drew the officer toward it. Once installed inside, he let the curtain drop till only a small loophole remained. The steps, which had been gradually growing louder, kept advancing; and presently they could hear the intruder's breathing, which was both quick and labored.

"Does he know that any one has entered the house? Did he see you when you came upon him upstairs?" whispered Mr. Gryce into the ear of the man beside him.

Styles shook his head, and pointed eagerly toward the opposite door. The man for whose appearance they waited had just lifted the portière and in another moment stood in full view just inside the threshold.

Mr. Gryce and his attendant colleague both stared. Was this the murderer? This pale, lean servitor, with a tray in his hand on which rested a single glass of water?

Mr. Gryce was so astonished that he looked at Styles for explanation. But that officer, hiding his own surprise, for he had not expected this peaceful figure, urged him in a whisper to have patience, and both, turning toward the man again, beheld him advance, stop, cast one look at the figure lying on the floor and then let slip the glass with a low cry that at once changed to something like a howl.

"Look at him! Look at him!" urged Styles, in a hurried whisper. "Watch what he will do now. You will see a murderer at work."

And sure enough, in another instant this strange being, losing all semblance to his former self, entered upon a series of pantomimic actions which to the two men who watched him seemed both to explain and illustrate the crime which had just been enacted there.

With every appearance of passion, he stood contemplating the empty air before him, and then, with one hand held stretched out behind him in a peculiarly cramped position, he plunged with the other toward a table from which he made a feint of snatching something which he no sooner closed his hand upon than he gave a quick side-thrust, still at the empty air, which seemed to quiver in return, so vigorous was his action and so evident his intent.

The reaction following this thrust; the slow unclosing of his hand from an imaginary dagger; the tottering of his body backward; then the moment when with wide open eyes he seemed to contemplate in horror the result of his own deed;—these needed no explanation beyond what was given by his writhing features and trembling body. Gradually succumbing to the remorse or terror of his own crime, he sank lower and lower, until, though with that one arm still stretched out, he lay in an inert heap on the floor.

"It is what I saw him do upstairs," murmured Styles into the ear of the amazed detective. "He has evidently been driven insane by his own act."

Mr. Gryce made no answer. Here was a problem for the solution of which he found no precedent in all his past experience.

CHAPTER III

THE MUTE SERVITOR

Meanwhile the man who, to all appearance, had just re-enacted before them the tragedy which had so lately taken place in this room, rose to his feet, and, with a dazed air as unlike his former violent expression as possible, stooped for the glass he had let fall, and was carrying it out when Mr. Gryce called to him:

"Wait, man! You needn't take that glass away. We first want to hear how your master comes to be lying here dead."

It was a demand calculated to startle any man. But this one showed himself totally unmoved by it, and was passing on when Styles laid a detaining hand on his shoulder.

"Stop!" said he. "What do you mean by sliding off like this? Don't you hear the gentleman speaking to you?"

This time the appeal told. The glass fell again from the man's hand, mingling its clink (for it struck the floor this time and broke) with the cry he gave—which was not exactly a cry either, but an odd sound between a moan and a shriek. He had caught sight of the men who were seeking to detain him, and his haggard look and cringing form showed that he realized at last the terrors of his position. Next minute he sought to escape, but Styles, gripping him more firmly, dragged him back to where Mr. Gryce stood beside the bearskin rug on which lay the form of his dead master.

Instantly, at the sight of this recumbent figure, another change took place in the entrapped butler. Joy—that most hellish of passions in the presence of violence and death—illumined his wandering eye and distorted his mouth; and, seeking no disguise for the satisfaction he felt, he uttered a low but thrilling laugh, which rang in unholy echo through the room.

Mr. Gryce, moved in spite of himself by an abhorrence which the irresponsible condition of this man seemed only to emphasize, waited till the last faint sounds of this diabolical mirth had died away in the high recesses of the space above. Then, fixing the glittering eye of this strange creature with his own, which, as we know, so seldom dwelt upon that of his fellow-beings, he sternly said:

"There now! Speak! Who killed this man? You were in the house with him, and should know."

The butler's lips opened and a string of strange gutturals poured forth, while with his one disengaged hand (for the other was held to his side by Styles) he touched his ears and his lips, and violently shook his head.

There was but one interpretation to be given to this. The man was deaf and dumb.

The shock of this discovery was too much for Styles. His hand fell from the other's arms, and the man, finding himself free, withdrew to his former place in the room, where he proceeded to enact again and with increased vivacity first the killing of and then the mourning for his master, which but a few moments before had made so suggestive an impression upon them. This done, he stood waiting, but this time with that gleam of infernal joy in the depths of his quick, restless eyes which made his very presence in this room of death seem a sacrilege and horror.

Styles could not stand it. "Can't you speak?" he shouted. "Can't you hear?"

The man only smiled, an evil and gloating smile, which Mr. Gryce thought it his duty to cut short.

"Take him away!" he cried. "Examine him carefully for blood marks. I am going up to the room where you saw him first. He is too nearly linked to this crime not to carry some trace of it away with him."

But for once even this time-tried detective found himself at fault. No marks were found on the old servant, nor could they discover in the rooms above any signs by which this one remaining occupant of the house could be directly associated with the crime which had taken place within it. Thereupon Mr. Gryce grew very thoughtful and entered upon another examination of the two rooms which to his mind held all the clews that would ever be given to this strange crime.

The result was meagre, and he was just losing himself again in contemplation of the upturned face, whose fixed mouth and haunting expression told such a story of suffering and determination, when there came from the dim recesses above his head a cry, which, forming itself into two words, rang down with startling clearness in this most unexpected of appeals:

"Remember Evelyn!"

Remember Evelyn! Who was Evelyn? And to whom did this voice belong, in a house which had already been ransacked in vain for other occupants? It seemed to come from the roof, and, sure enough, when Mr. Gryce looked up he saw, swinging in a cage strung up nearly to the top of one of the windows I have mentioned, an English starling, which, in seeming recognition of the attention it had drawn upon itself, craned its neck as Mr. Gryce looked up, and shrieked again, with fiercer insistence than before:

"Remember Evelyn!"

It was the last uncanny touch in a series of uncanny experiences. With an odd sense of nightmare upon him, Mr. Gryce leaned forward on the study table in his effort to obtain a better view of this bird, when, without warning, the white light, which since his last contact with the electrical apparatus had spread itself through the room, changed again to green, and he realized that he had unintentionally pressed a button and thus brought into action another slide in the curious lamp over his head.

Annoyed, for these changing hues offered a problem he was as yet too absorbed in other matters to make any attempt to solve, he left the vicinity of the table, and was about to leave the room when he heard Styles's voice rise from the adjoining antechamber, where Styles was keeping guard over the old butler:

"Shall I let him go, Mr. Gryce? He seems very uneasy; not dangerous, you know, but anxious; as if he had forgotten something or recalled some unfulfilled duty."

"Yes, let him go," was the detective's quick reply. "Only watch and follow him. Every movement he makes is of interest.

Unconsciously he may be giving us invaluable clews." And he approached the door to note for himself what the man might do.

"Remember Evelyn!" rang out the startling cry from above, as the detective passed between the curtains. Irresistibly he looked back and up. To whom was this appeal from a bird's throat so imperatively addressed? To him or to the man on the floor beneath, whose ears were forever closed? It might be a matter of little consequence, and it might be one involving the very secret of this tragedy. But whether important or not, he could pay no heed to it at this juncture, for the old butler, coming from the front hall whither he had hurried on being released by Styles, was at that moment approaching him, carrying in one hand his master's hat and in the other his master's umbrella.

Not knowing what this new movement might mean, Mr. Gryce paused where he was and waited for the man to advance. Seeing this, the mute, to whose face and bearing had returned the respectful immobility of the trained servant, handed over the articles he had brought, and then noiselessly, and with the air of one who had performed an expected service, retreated to his old place in the antechamber, where he sat down again and fell almost immediately into his former dazed condition.

"Humph! mind quite lost, memory uncertain, testimony valueless," were the dissatisfied reflections of the disappointed detective as he replaced Mr. Adams's hat and umbrella on the hall rack. "Has he been brought to this state by the tragedy which has just taken place here, or is his present insane condition its precursor and cause?" Mr. Gryce might have found some answer to this question in his own mind if, at that moment, the fitful clanging of the front door bell, which had hitherto testified to the impatience of the curious crowd outside, had not been broken into by an authoritative knock which at once put an end to all self-communing.

The coroner, or some equally important person, was at hand, and the detective's golden hour was over.

CHAPTER IV

A NEW EXPERIENCE FOR MR. GRYCE

Mr. Gryce felt himself at a greater disadvantage in his attempt to solve the mystery of this affair than in any other which he had entered upon in years. First, the victim had been a solitary man, with no household save his man-of-all-work, the mute. Secondly, he had lived in a portion of the city where no neighbors were possible; and he had even lacked, as it now seemed, any very active friends. Though some hours had elapsed since his death had been noised abroad, no one had appeared at the door with inquiries or information. This seemed odd, considering that he had been for some months a marked figure in this quarter of the town. But, then, everything about this man was odd, nor would it have been in keeping with his surroundings and peculiar manner of living for him to have had the ordinary associations of men of his class.

This absence of the usual means of eliciting knowledge from the surrounding people, added to, rather than detracted from, the interest which Mr. Gryce was bound to feel in the case, and it was with a feeling of relief that a little before midnight he saw the army of reporters, medical men, officials, and such others as had followed in the coroner's wake, file out of the front door and leave him again, for a few hours at least, master of the situation.

For there were yet two points which he desired to settle before he took his own much-needed rest. The first occupied his immediate attention. Passing before a chair in the hall on which a small boy sat dozing, he roused him with the remark:

"Come, Jake, it's time to look lively. I want you to go with me to the exact place where that lady ran across you to-day."

The boy, half dead with sleep, looked around him for his hat.

"I'd like to see my mother first," he pleaded. "She must be done up about me. I never stayed away so long before."

"Your mother knows where you are. I sent a message to her hours ago. She gave a very good report of you, Jake; says you're an obedient lad and that you never have told her a falsehood."

"She's a good mother," the boy warmly declared. "I'd be as bad— as bad as my father was, if I did not treat her well." Here his hand fell on his cap, which he put on his head.

"I'm ready," said he.

Mr. Gryce at once led the way into the street.

The hour was late, and only certain portions of the city showed any real activity. Into one of these thoroughfares they presently came, and before the darkened window of one of the lesser shops paused, while Jake pointed out the two stuffed frogs engaged with miniature swords in mortal combat at which he had been looking when the lady came up and spoke to him.

Mr. Gryce eyed the boy rather than the frogs, though probably the former would have sworn that his attention had never left that miniature conflict.

"Was she a pretty lady?" he asked.

The boy scratched his head in some perplexity.

"She made me a good deal afraid of her," he said. "She had very splendid clothes; oh, gorgeous!" he cried, as if on this question there could be no doubt.

"And she was young, and carried a bunch of flowers, and seemed troubled? What! not young, and carried no flowers—and wasn't even anxious and trembling?"

The boy, who had been shaking his head, looked nonplussed.

"I think as she was what you might call troubled. But she wasn't crying, and when she spoke to me, she put more feeling into her grip than into her voice. She just dragged me to the drug-store, sir. If she hadn't given me money first, I should have wriggled away in spite of her. But I likes money, sir; I don't get too much of it."

Mr. Gryce by this time was moving on. "Not young," he repeated to himself. "Some old flame, then, of Mr. Adams; they're apt to be dangerous, very dangerous, more dangerous than the young ones."

In front of the drug-store he paused. "Show me where she stood while you went in."

The boy pointed out the identical spot. He seemed as eager as the detective.

"And was she standing there when you came out?"

"Oh, no, sir; she went away while I was inside."

"Did you see her go? Can you tell me whether she went up street or down?"

"I had one eye on her, sir; I was afraid she was coming into the shop after me, and my arm was too sore for me to want her to clinch hold on it again. So when she started to go, I took a step nearer, and saw her move toward the curbstone and hold up her hand. But it wasn't a car she was after, for none came by for several minutes."

The fold between Mr. Gryce's eyes perceptibly smoothed out.

"Then it was some cabman or hack-driver she hailed. Were there any empty coaches about that you saw?"

The boy had not noticed. He had reached the limit of his observations, and no amount of further questioning could elicit anything more from him. This Mr. Gryce soon saw, and giving him into the charge of one of his assistants who was on duty at this place, he proceeded back to the ill-omened house where the tragedy itself had occurred.

"Any one waiting for me?" he inquired of Styles, who came to the door.

"Yes, sir; a young man; name, Hines. Says he's an electrician."

"That's the man I want. Where is he?"

"In the parlor, sir."

"Good! I'll see him. But don't let any one else in. Anybody upstairs?"

"No, sir, all gone. Shall I go up or stay here?"

"You'd better go up. I'll look after the door."

Styles nodded, and went toward the stairs, up which he presently disappeared. Mr. Gryce proceeded to the parlor.

A dapper young man with an intelligent eye rose to meet him. "You sent for me," said he.

The detective nodded, asked a few questions, and seeming satisfied with the replies he received, led the way into Mr. Adams's study, from which the body had been removed to an upper room. As they entered, a mild light greeted them from a candle which, by Mr. Gryce's orders, had been placed on a small side table near the door. But once in, Mr. Gryce approached the larger table in the centre of the room, and placing his hand on one of the buttons before him, asked his companion to be kind enough to blow out the candle. This he did, leaving the room for a moment in total darkness. Then with a sudden burst of illumination, a marvellous glow of a deep violet color shot over the whole room, and the two men turned and faced each other both with inquiry in their looks, so unexpected was this theatrical effect to the one, and so inexplicable its cause and purpose to the other.

"That is but one slide," remarked Mr. Gryce. "Now I will press another button, and the color changes to—pink, as you see. This one produces green, this one white, and this a bilious yellow, which is not becoming to either of us, I am sure. Now will you examine the connection, and see if there is anything peculiar about it?"

Mr. Hines at once set to work. But beyond the fact that the whole contrivance was the work of an amateur hand, he found nothing strange about it, except the fact that it worked so well.

Mr. Gryce showed disappointment.

"He made it, then, himself?" he asked.

"Undoubtedly, or some one else equally unacquainted with the latest method of wiring."

"Will you look at these books over here and see if sufficient knowledge can be got from them to enable an amateur to rig up such an arrangement as this?"

Mr. Hines glanced at the shelf which Mr. Gryce had pointed out, and without taking out the books, answered briefly:

"A man with a deft hand and a scientific turn of mind might, by the aid of these, do all you see here and more. The aptitude is all."

"Then I'm afraid Mr. Adams had the aptitude," was the dry response. There was disappointment in the tone. Why, his next words served to show. "A man with a turn for mechanical contrivances often wastes much time and money on useless toys only fit for children to play with. Look at that bird cage now. Perched at a height totally beyond the reach of any one without a ladder, it must owe its very evident usefulness (for you see it holds a rather lively occupant) to some contrivance by which it can be raised and lowered at will. Where is that contrivance? Can you find it?"

The expert thought he could. And, sure enough, after some ineffectual searching, he came upon another button well hid amid the tapestry on the wall, which, when pressed, caused something to be disengaged which gradually lowered the cage within reach of Mr. Gryce's hand.

"We will not send this poor bird aloft again," said he, detaching the cage and holding it for a moment in his hand. "An English starling is none too common in this country. Hark! he is going to speak."

But the sharp-eyed bird, warned perhaps by the emphatic gesture of the detective that silence would be more in order at this moment than his usual appeal to "remember Evelyn," whisked about in his cage for an instant, and then subsided into a doze, which may have been real, and may have been assumed under the fascinating eye of the old gentleman who held him. Mr. Gryce placed the cage on the floor, and idly, or because the play pleased him, old and staid as he was, pressed another button on the table—a button he had hitherto neglected touching—and glanced around to see what color the light would now assume.

But the yellow glare remained. The investigation which the apparatus had gone through had probably disarranged the wires. With a shrug he was moving off, when he suddenly made a hurried gesture, directing the attention of the expert to a fact for which neither of them was prepared. The opening which led into the antechamber, and which was the sole means of communication with the rest of the house, was slowly closing. From a yard's breadth it became a foot; from a foot it became an inch; from an inch——

"Well, that is certainly the contrivance of a lazy man," laughed the expert. "Seated in his chair here, he can close his door at will. No shouting after a deaf servant, no awkward stumbling over rugs to shut it himself. I don't know but I approve of this contrivance, only——" here he caught a rather serious expression on Mr. Gryce's face—"the slide seems to be of a somewhat curious construction. It is not made of wood, as any sensible door ought to be, but of——"

"Steel," finished Mr. Gryce in an odd tone. "This is the strangest thing yet. It begins to look as if Mr. Adams was daft on electrical contrivances."

"And as if we were prisoners here," supplemented the other. "I do not see any means for drawing this slide back."

"Oh, there's another button for that, of course," Mr. Gryce carelessly remarked.

But they failed to find one.

"If you don't object," observed Mr. Gryce, after five minutes of useless search, "I will turn a more cheerful light upon the scene. Yellow does not seem to fit the occasion."

"Give us rose, for unless you have some one on the other side of this steel plate, we seem likely to remain here till morning."

"There is a man upstairs whom we may perhaps make hear, but what does this contrivance portend? It has a serious look to me, when you consider that every window in these two rooms has been built up almost under the roof."

"Yes; a very strange look. But before engaging in its consideration I should like a breath of fresh air. I cannot do anything while in confinement. My brain won't work."

Meanwhile Mr. Gryce was engaged in examining the huge plate of steel which served as a barrier to their egress. He found that it had been made—certainly at great expense—to fit the curve of the walls through which it passed. This was a discovery of some consequence, causing Mr. Gryce to grow still more thoughtful and to eye the smooth steel plate under his hand with an air of marked distrust.

"Mr. Adams carried his taste for the mechanical to great extremes," he remarked to the slightly uneasy man beside him. "This slide is very carefully fitted, and, if I am not mistaken, it will stand some battering before we are released."

"I wish that his interest in electricity had led him to attach such a simple thing as a bell."

"True, we have come across no bell."

"It would have smacked too much of the ordinary to please him."

"Besides, his only servant was deaf."

"Try the effect of a blow, a quick blow with this silver-mounted alpenstock. Some one should hear and come to our assistance."

"I will try my whistle first; it will be better understood."

But though Mr. Gryce both whistled and struck many a resounding knock upon the barrier before them, it was an hour before he could draw the attention of Styles, and five hours before an opening could be effected in the wall large enough to admit of their escape, so firmly was this barrier of steel fixed across the sole outlet from this remarkable room.

CHAPTER V

FIVE SMALL SPANGLES

Such an experience could not fail to emphasize Mr. Gryce's interest in the case and heighten the determination he had formed to probe its secrets and explain all its extraordinary features. Arrived at Headquarters, where his presence was doubtless awaited with some anxiety by those who knew nothing of the cause of his long detention, his first act was to inquire if Bartow, the butler, had come to his senses during the night.

The answer was disappointing. Not only was there no change in his condition, but the expert in lunacy who had been called in to pass upon his case had expressed an opinion unfavorable to his immediate recovery.

Mr. Gryce looked sober, and, summoning the officer who had managed Bartow's arrest, he asked how the mute had acted when he found himself detained.

The answer was curt, but very much to the point.

"Surprised, sir. Shook his head and made some queer gestures, then went through his pantomime. It's quite a spectacle, sir. Poor fool, he keeps holding his hand back, so."

Mr. Gryce noted the gesture; it was the same which Bartow had made when he first realized that he had spectators. Its meaning was not wholly apparent. He had made it with his right hand (there was no evidence that the mute was left-handed), and he continued to make it as if with this movement he expected to call attention to some fact that would relieve him from custody.

"Does he mope? Is his expression one of fear or anger?"

"It varies, sir. One minute he looks like a man on the point of falling asleep; the next he starts up in fury, shaking his head and pounding the walls. It's not a comfortable sight, sir. He will have to be watched night and day."

"Let him be, and note every change in him. His testimony may not be valid, but there is suggestion in every movement he makes. To-morrow I will visit him myself."

The officer went out, and Mr. Gryce sat for a few moments communing with himself, during which he took out a little package from his pocket, and emptying out on his desk the five little spangles it contained, regarded them intently. He had always been fond of looking at some small and seemingly insignificant object while thinking. It served to concentrate his thoughts, no doubt. At all events, some such result appeared to follow the contemplation of these five sequins, for after shaking his head doubtfully over them for a time, he made a sudden move, and sweeping them into the envelope from which he had taken them, he gave a glance at his watch and passed quickly into the outer office, where he paused before a line of waiting men. Beckoning to one who had followed his movements with an interest which had not escaped the eye of this old reader of human nature, he led the way back to his own room.

"You want a hand in this matter?" he said interrogatively, as the door closed behind them and they found themselves alone.

"Oh, sir—" began the young man in a glow which made his more than plain features interesting to contemplate, "I do not presume——"

"Enough!" interposed the other. "You have been here now for six months, and have had no opportunity as yet for showing any special adaptability. Now I propose to test your powers with something really difficult. Are you up to it, Sweetwater? Do you know the city well enough to attempt to find a needle in this very big haystack?"

"I should at least like to try," was the eager response. "If I succeed it will be a bigger feather in my cap than if I had always lived in New York. I have been spoiling for some such opportunity. See if I don't make the effort judiciously, if only out of gratitude."

"Well, we shall see," remarked the old detective. "If it's difficulty you long to encounter, you will be likely to have all you want of it.

Indeed, it is the impossible I ask. A woman is to be found of whom we know nothing save that she wore when last seen a dress heavily bespangled with black, and that she carried in her visit to Mr. Adams, at the time of or before the murder, a parasol, of which I can procure you a glimpse before you start out. She came from, I don't know where, and she went—but that is what you are to find out. You are not the only man who is to be put on the job, which, as you see, is next door to a hopeless one, unless the woman comes forward and proclaims herself. Indeed, I should despair utterly of your success if it were not for one small fact which I will now proceed to give you as my special and confidential agent in this matter. When this woman was about to disappear from the one eye that was watching her, she approached the curbstone in front of Hudson's fruit store on 14th Street and lifted up her right hand, so. It is not much of a clew, but it is all I have at my disposal, except these five spangles dropped from her dress, and my conviction that she is not to be found among the questionable women of the town, but among those who seldom or never come under the eye of the police. Yet don't let this conviction hamper you. Convictions as a rule are bad things, and act as a hindrance rather than an inspiration."

Sweetwater, to whom the song of the sirens would have sounded less sweet, listened with delight and responded with a frank smile and a gay:

"I'll do my best, sir, but don't show me the parasol, only describe it. I wouldn't like the fellows to chaff me if I fail; I'd rather go quietly to work and raise no foolish expectations."

"Well, then, it is one of those dainty, nonsensical things made of gray chiffon, with pearl handle and bows of pink ribbon. I don't believe it was ever used before, and from the value women usually place on such fol-de-rols, could only have been left behind under the stress of extraordinary emotion or fear. The name of the owner was not on it."

"Nor that of the maker?"

Mr. Gryce had expected this question, and was glad not to be disappointed.

"No, that would have helped us too much."

"And the hour at which this lady was seen on the curbstone at Hudson's?"

"Half-past four; the moment at which the telephone message arrived."

"Very good, sir. It is the hardest task I have ever undertaken, but that's not against it. When shall I see you again?"

"When you have something to impart. Ah, wait a minute. I have my suspicion that this woman's first name is Evelyn. But, mind, it is only a suspicion."

"All right, sir," and with an air of some confidence, the young man disappeared.

Mr. Gryce did not look as if he shared young Sweetwater's cheerfulness. The mist surrounding this affair was as yet impenetrable to him. But then he was not twenty-three, with only triumphant memories behind him.

His next hope lay in the information likely to accrue from the published accounts of this crime, now spread broadcast over the country. A man of Mr. Adams's wealth and culture must necessarily have possessed many acquaintances, whom the surprising news of his sudden death would naturally bring to light, especially as no secret was made of his means and many valuable effects. But as if this affair, destined to be one of the last to engage the powers of this sagacious old man, refused on this very account to yield any immediate results to his investigation, the whole day passed by without the appearance of any claimant for Mr. Adams's fortune or the arrival on the scene of any friend capable of lifting the veil which shrouded the life of this strange being. To be sure, his banker and his lawyer came forward during the day, but they had little to reveal beyond the fact that his pecuniary affairs were in good shape and that, so far as they knew, he was without family or kin.

Even his landlord could add little to the general knowledge. He had first heard of Mr. Adams through a Philadelphia lawyer, since dead, who had assured him of his client's respectability and undoubted ability to pay his rent. When they came together and Mr. Adams was introduced to him, he had been struck, first, by the ascetic appearance of his prospective tenant, and, secondly, by his reserved manners and quiet intelligence. But admirable as he had found him, he had never succeeded in making his acquaintance. The rent had been uniformly paid with great exactitude on the very day it was due, but his own visits had never been encouraged or his advances met by anything but the cold politeness of a polished and totally indifferent man. Indeed, he had always looked upon his tenant as a bookworm, absorbed in study and such scientific experiments as could be carried on with no other assistance than that of his deaf and dumb servant.

Asked if he knew anything about this servant, he answered that his acquaintance with him was limited to the two occasions on which he had been ushered by him into his master's presence; that he knew nothing of his character and general disposition, and could not say whether his attitude toward his master had been one of allegiance or antagonism.

And so the way was blocked in this direction.

Taken into the room where Mr. Adams had died, he surveyed in amazement the huge steel plate which still blocked the doorway, and the high windows through which only a few straggling sunbeams could find their way.

Pointing to the windows, he remarked:

"These were filled in at Mr. Adams's request. Originally they extended down to the wainscoting."

He was shown where lath and plaster had been introduced and also how the plate had been prepared and arranged as a barrier. But he could give no explanation of it or divine the purpose for which it had been placed there at so great an expense.

The lamp was another curiosity, and its varying lights the cause of increased astonishment. Indeed he had known nothing of these arrangements, having been received in the parlor when he visited the house, where there was nothing to attract his attention or emphasize the well-known oddities of his tenant.

He was not shown the starling. That loquacious bird had been removed to police headquarters for the special delectation of Mr. Gryce.

Other inquiries failed also. No clew to the owner of the insignia found on the wall could be gained at the pension office or at any of the G. A. R. posts inside the city. Nor was the name of the artist who had painted the portrait which adorned so large a portion of the wall a recognized one in New York City. Otherwise a clew might have been obtained through him to Mr. Adams's antecedents. All the drawers and receptacles in Mr. Adams's study had been searched, but no will had been found nor any business documents. It was as if this strange man had sought to suppress his identity, or, rather, as if he had outgrown all interest in his kind or in anything beyond the walls within which he had immured himself.

Late in the afternoon reports began to come in from the various tradesmen with whom Mr. Adams had done business. They all had something to say as to the peculiarity of his habits and the freaks of his mute servant. They were both described as hermits, differing from the rest of their kind only in that they denied themselves no reasonable luxury and seemed to have adopted a shut-in life from a pure love of seclusion. The master was never seen at the stores. It was the servant who made the purchases, and this by means of gestures which were often strangely significant. Indeed, he seemed to have great power of expressing himself by looks and actions, and rarely caused a mistake or made one. He would not endure cheating, and always bought the best.

Of his sanity up to the day of his master's death there was no question; but more than one man with whom he had had dealings was ready to testify that there had been a change in his manner for the past few weeks—a sort of subdued excitement, quite unlike his former methodical bearing. He had shown an inclination to testiness, and was less easily pleased than formerly. To one clerk he had shown a nasty spirit under very slight provocation, and was only endured in the store on account of his master, who was too good a customer for them to offend. Mr. Kelly, a grocer, went so far as to say he acted like a man with a grievance who burned to vent his spite on some one, but held himself in forcible restraint.

Perhaps if no tragedy had taken place in the house on —— Street these various persons would not have been so ready to interpret thus unfavorably a nervousness excusable enough in one so cut off from all communication with his kind. But with the violent end of his master in view, and his own unexplained connection with it, who could help recalling that his glance had frequently shown malevolence?

But this was not evidence of the decided character required by the law, and Mr. Gryce was about to regard the day as a lost one, when Sweetwater made his reappearance at Headquarters. The expression of his face put new life into Mr. Gryce.

"What!" he cried, "you have not found her?"

Sweetwater smiled. "Don't ask me, sir, not yet. I've come to see if there's any reason why I should not be given the loan of that parasol for about an hour. I'll bring it back. I only want to make a certain test with it."

"What test, my boy? May I ask, what test?"

"Please to excuse me, sir; I have only a short time in which to act before respectable business houses shut up for the night, and the test I speak of has to be made in a respectable house."

"Then you shall not be hindered. Wait here, and I will bring you the parasol. There! bring it back soon, my boy. I have not the patience I used to have."

"An hour, sir; give me an hour, and then——"

The shutting of the door behind his flying figure cut short his sentence.

That was a long hour to Mr. Gryce, or would have been if it had not mercifully been cut short by the return of Sweetwater in an even more excited state of mind than he had been before. He held the parasol in his hand.

"My test failed," said he, "but the parasol has brought me luck, notwithstanding. I have found the lady, sir, and——"

He had to draw a long breath before proceeding.

"And she is what I said," began the detective; "a respectable person in a respectable house."

"Yes, sir; very respectable, more respectable than I expected to see. Quite a lady, sir. Not young, but——"

"Her name, boy. Is it—Evelyn?"

Sweetwater shook his head with a look as naive in its way as the old detective's question.

"I cannot say, sir. Indeed, I had not the courage to ask. She is here——"

"Here!" Mr. Gryce took one hurried step toward the door, then came gravely back. "I can restrain myself," he said. "If she is here, she will not go till I have seen her. Are you sure you have made no mistake; that she is the woman we are after; the woman who was in Mr. Adams's house and sent us the warning?"

"Will you hear my story, sir? It will take only a moment. Then you can judge for yourself."

"Your story? It must be a pretty one. How came you to light on this woman so soon? By using the clew I gave you?"

Again Sweetwater's expression took on a touch of naïveté.

"I'm sorry, sir; but I was egotistical enough to follow my own idea. It would have taken too much time to hunt up all the drivers of hacks in the city, and I could not even be sure she had made use of a public conveyance. No, sir; I bethought me of another way by which I might reach this woman. You had shown me those spangles. They were portions of a very rich trimming; a trimming which has only lately come into vogue, and which is so expensive that it is worn chiefly by women of means, and sold only in shops where elaborate garnitures are to be found. I have seen and noticed dresses thus trimmed, in certain windows and on certain ladies; and before you showed me the spangles you picked up in Mr. Adams's study could have told you just how I had seen them arranged. They are sewed on black net, in figures, sir; in scrolls or wreaths or whatever you choose to call them; and so conspicuous are these wreaths or figures, owing to the brilliance of the spangles composing them, that any break in their continuity is plainly apparent, especially if the net be worn over a color, as is frequently the case. Remembering this, and recalling the fact that these spangles doubtless fell from one of the front breadths, where their loss would attract not only the attention of others, but that of the wearer, I said to myself, 'What will she be likely to do when she finds her dress thus disfigured?' And the answer at once came: 'If she is the lady Mr. Gryce considers her, she will seek to restore these missing spangles, especially if they were lost on a scene of crime. But where can she get them to sew on? From an extra piece of net of the same style. But she will not be apt to have an extra piece of net. She will, therefore, find herself obliged to buy it, and since only a few spangles are lacking, she will buy the veriest strip.' Here, then, was my clew, or at least my ground for action. Going the rounds of the few leading stores on Broadway, 23d Street, and Sixth Avenue, I succeeded in getting certain clerks interested in my efforts, so that I speedily became assured that if a lady came into these stores for a very small portion of this bespangled net, they would note her person and, if possible, procure some clew to her address. Then I took up my stand at Arnold's emporium. Why Arnold's? I do not know. Perhaps my good genius meant me to be successful in this quest; but whether through luck or what not, I was successful, for before the afternoon was half over, I encountered a meaning glance from one of the men behind the counter, and advancing toward him, saw him rolling a small package which he handed over to a very pretty and rosy young girl, who at once walked away with it. 'For one of our leading customers,' he whispered, as I drew nearer. 'I don't think she is the person you want.' But I would take no chances. I followed the young girl who had carried away the parcel, and by this means came to a fine brownstone front in one of our most retired and aristocratic quarters. When I had seen her go in at the basement door, I rang the bell above, and then—well, I just bit my lips to keep down my growing excitement. For such an effort as this might well end in disappointment, and I knew if I were disappointed now—But no such trial awaited me. The maid who came to the door proved to be the same merry-eyed lass I had seen leave the store. Indeed, she had the identical parcel in her hand which was the connecting link between the imposing house at whose door I stood and the strange murder in —— Street. But I did not allow my interest in this parcel to become apparent, and by the time I addressed her I had so mastered myself as to arouse no suspicion of the importance of my errand. You, of course, foresee the question I put to the young girl. 'Has your mistress lost a parasol? One has been found—' I did not finish the sentence, for I perceived by her look that her mistress had met with such a loss, and as this was all I wanted to know just then, I cried out, 'I will bring it. If it is hers, all right,' and bounded down the steps.

"My intention was to inform you of what I had done and ask your advice. But my egotism got the better of me. I felt that I ought to make sure that I was not the victim of a coincidence. Such a respectable house! Such a respectable maidservant! Should she recognize the parasol as belonging to her mistress, then, indeed, I might boast of my success. So praying you for a loan of this article, I went back and rang the bell again. The same girl came to the door. I think fortune favored me to-day. 'Here is the parasol,' said I, but before the words were out of my mouth I saw that the girl had taken the alarm or that some grievous mistake had been made. 'That is not the one my mistress lost,' said she. 'She never carries anything but black.' And the door was about to close between us when I heard a voice from within call out peremptorily: 'Let me see that parasol. Hold it up, young man. There! at the foot of the stairs. Ah!'

"If ever an exclamation was eloquent that simple 'ah!' was. I could not see the speaker, but I knew she was leaning over the banisters from the landing above. I listened to hear her glide away. But she did not move. She was evidently collecting herself for the emergency of the moment. Presently she spoke again, and I was astonished at her tone: 'You have come from Police Headquarters,' was the remark with which she hailed me.

"I lowered the parasol. I did not think it necessary to say yes.

"'From a man there, called Gryce,' she went on, still in that strange tone I can hardly describe, sir.

"'Since you ask me,' I now replied, 'I acknowledge that it is through his instructions I am here. He was anxious to restore to you your lost property. Is not this parasol yours? Shall I not leave it with this young girl?'

"The answer was dry, almost rasping: 'Mr. Gryce has made a mistake. The parasol is not mine; yet he certainly deserves credit for the use he has made of it, in this search. I should like to tell him so. Is he at his office, and do you think I would be received?'

"'He would be delighted,' I returned, not imagining she was in earnest. But she was, sir. In less time than you would believe, I perceived a very stately, almost severe, lady descend the stairs. She was dressed for the street, and spoke to me with quite an air of command. 'Have you a cab?' she asked.

"'No,' said I.

"'Then get one.'

"Here was a dilemma. Should I leave her and thus give her an opportunity to escape, or should I trust to her integrity and the honesty of her look, which was no common one, sir, and obey her as every one about her was evidently accustomed to do?

"I concluded to trust to her integrity, and went for the cab. But it was a risk, sir, which I promise not to repeat in the future. She was awaiting me on the stoop when I got back, and at once entered the hack with a command to drive immediately to Police Headquarters. I saw her as I came in just now sitting in the outer office, waiting for you. Are you ready to say I have done well?"

Mr. Gryce, with an indescribable look of mingled envy and indulgence, pressed the hand held out to him, and passed out. His curiosity could be restrained no longer, and he went at once to where this mysterious woman was awaiting him. Did he think it odd that she knew him, that she sought him? If so, he did not betray this in his manner, which was one of great respect. But that manner suddenly changed as he came face to face with the lady in question. Not that it lost its respect, but that it betrayed an astonishment of a more pronounced character than was usually indulged in by this experienced detective. The lady before him was one well known to him; in fact, almost an associate of his in certain bygone matters; in other words, none other than that most reputable of ladies, Miss Amelia Butterworth of Gramercy Park.

CHAPTER VI

SUGGESTIONS FROM AN OLD FRIEND

The look with which this amiable spinster met his eye was one which a stranger would have found it hard to understand. He found it hard to understand himself, perhaps because he had never before seen this lady when she was laboring under an opinion of herself that was not one of perfect complacency.

"Miss Butterworth! What does this mean? Have you——"

"There!" The word came with some sharpness. "You have detected me at my old tricks, and I am correspondingly ashamed, and you triumphant. The gray parasol you have been good enough to send to my house is not mine, but I was in the room where you picked it up, as you have so cleverly concluded, and as it is useless for me to evade your perspicacity, I have come here to confess."

"Ah!" The detective was profoundly interested at once. He drew a chair up to Miss Butterworth's side and sat down. "You were there!" he repeated; "and when? I do not presume to ask for what purpose."

"But I shall have to explain my purpose not to find myself at too great a disadvantage," she replied with grim decision. "Not that I like to display my own weakness, but that I recognize the exigencies of the occasion, and fully appreciate your surprise at finding that I, a stranger to Mr. Adams, and without the excuse which led to my former interference in police matters, should have so far forgotten myself as to be in my present position before you. This was no affair of my immediate neighbor, nor did it seek me. I sought it, sir, and in this way. I wish I had gone to Jericho first; it might have meant longer travel and much more expense; but it would have involved me in less humiliation and possible publicity. Mr. Gryce, I never meant to be mixed up with another murder case. I have shown my aptitude for detective work and received, ere now, certain marks of your approval; but my head was not turned by them—at least I thought not—and I was tolerably sincere in my determination to keep to my own *metier* in future and not suffer myself to be allured by any inducements you might offer into the exercise of gifts which may have brought me praise in the past, but certainly have not brought me happiness. But the temptation came, not through you, or I might have resisted it, but through a combination of circumstances which found me weak, and, in a measure, unprepared. In other words, I was surprised into taking an interest in this affair. Oh, I am ashamed of it, so ashamed that I have made the greatest endeavor to hide my participation in the matter, and thinking I had succeeded in doing so, was congratulating myself upon my precautions, when I found that parasol thrust in my face and realized that you, if no one else, knew that Amelia Butterworth had been in Mr. Adams's room of death prior to yourself. Yet I thought I had left no traces behind me. Could you have seen——"

"Miss Butterworth, you dropped five small spangles from your robe. You wore a dress spangled with black sequins, did you not? Besides, you moved the inkstand, and—Well, I will never put faith in circumstantial evidence again. I saw these tokens of a woman's presence, heard what the boy had to say of the well-dressed lady who had sent him into the drug-store with a message to the police, and drew the conclusion—I may admit it to you—that it was this woman who had wielded the assassin's dagger, and not the deaf-and-dumb butler, who, until now, has borne the blame of it. Therefore I was anxious to find her, little realizing what would be the result of my efforts, or that I should have to proffer her my most humble apologies."

"Do not apologize to me. I had no business to be there, or, at least, to leave the five spangles you speak of, behind me on Mr. Adams's miserable floor. I was simply passing by the house; and had I been the woman I once was, that is, a woman who had never dipped into a mystery, I should have continued on my way, instead of turning aside. Sir, it's a curious sensation to find yourself, however innocent, regarded by a whole city full of people as the cause or motive of a terrible murder, especially when you have spent some time, as I have, in the study of crime and the pursuit of criminals. I own I don't enjoy the experience. But I have brought it on myself. If I had not been so curious—But it was not curiosity I felt. I will never own that I am subject to mere curiosity; it was the look on the young man's face. But I forget myself. I am rambling in all directions when I ought to be telling a consecutive tale. Not my usual habit, sir; this you know; but I am not quite myself at this moment. I declare I am more upset by this discovery of my indiscretion than I was by Mr. Trohm's declaration of affection in Lost Man's Lane! Give me time, Mr. Gryce; in a few minutes I will be more coherent."

"I am giving you time," he returned with one of his lowest bows. "The half-dozen questions I long to ask have not yet left my lips, and I sit here, as you must yourself acknowledge, a monument of patience."

"So you thought this deed perpetrated by an outsider," she suddenly broke in. "Most of the journals—I read them very carefully this morning—ascribed the crime to the man you have mentioned. And there seems to be good reason for doing so. The case is not a simple one, Mr. Gryce; it has complications—I recognized that at once, and that is why—but I won't waste another moment in apologies. You have a right to any little fact I may have picked up in my unfortunate visit, and there is one which I failed to find included in any account of the murder. Mr. Adams had other visitors besides myself in those few fatal minutes preceding his death. A young man and woman were with him. I saw them come out of the house. It was at the moment I was passing——"

"Tell your story more simply, Miss Butterworth. What first drew your attention to the house?"

"There! That is the second time you have had to remind me to be more direct. You will not have to do so again, Mr. Gryce. To begin, then, I noticed the house, because I always notice it. I never pass it without giving a thought to its ancient history and indulging in more or less speculation as to its present inmates. When, therefore, I found myself in front of it yesterday afternoon on my way to the art exhibition, I naturally looked up, and—whether by an act of providence or not, I cannot say—it was precisely at that instant the inner door of the vestibule burst open, and a young man appeared in the hall, carrying a young woman in his arms. He seemed to be in a state of intense excitement, and she in a dead faint; but before they had attracted the attention of the crowd, he had placed her on her feet, and, taking her on his arm, dragged her down the stoop and into the crowd of passers-by, among whom they presently disappeared. I, as you may believe, stood rooted to the ground in my astonishment, and not only endeavored to see in what direction they went, but lingered long enough to take a peep into the time-honored interior of this old house, which had been left open to view by the young man's forgetting to close the front door behind him. As I did so, I heard a cry from within. It was muffled and remote, but unmistakably one of terror and anguish: and, led by an impulse I may live to regret, as it seems likely to plunge me into much unpleasantness, I rushed up the stoop and went in, shutting the door behind me, lest others should be induced to follow.

"So far, I had acted solely from instinct; but once in that semi-dark hall, I paused and asked what business I had there, and what excuse I should give for my intrusion if I encountered one or more of the occupants of the house. But a repetition of the cry, coming as I am ready to swear from the farthest room on the parlor floor, together with a sharp remembrance of the wandering eye and drawn countenance of the young man whom I had seen stagger hence a moment before, with an almost fainting woman in his arms, drew me on in spite of my feminine instincts; and before I knew it, I was in the circular study and before the prostrate form of a seemingly dying man. He was lying as you probably found him a little later, with the cross on his breast and a dagger in his heart; but his right hand was trembling, and when I stooped to lift his head, he gave a shudder and then settled into eternal stillness. I, a stranger from the street, had witnessed his last breath while the young man who had gone out——"

"Can you describe him? Did you encounter him close enough for recognition?"

"Yes, I think I would know him again. I can at least describe his appearance. He wore a checked suit, very natty, and was more than usually tall and fine-looking. But his chief peculiarity lay in his expression. I never saw on any face, no, not on the stage, at the climax of the most heart-rending tragedy, a greater accumulation of mortal passion struggling with the imperative necessity for restraint. The young girl whose blond head lay on his shoulder looked like a saint in the clutch of a demon. She had seen death, but he—But I prefer not to be the interpreter of that expressive countenance. It was lost to my view almost immediately, and probably calmed itself in the face of the throng he entered, or we would be hearing about him to-day. The girl seemed to be devoid of almost all feeling. I should not remember her."

"And was that all? Did you just look at that recumbent man and vanish? Didn't you encounter the butler? Haven't you some definite knowledge to impart in his regard which will settle his innocence or fix his guilt?"

"I know no more about him than you do, sir, except that he was not in the room by the time I reached it, and did not come into it during my presence there. Yet it was his cry that led me to the spot; or do you think it was that of the bird I afterward heard shouting and screaming in the cage over the dead man's head?"

"It might have been the bird," admitted Mr. Gryce. "Its call is very clear, and it seems strangely intelligent. What was it saying while you stood there?"

"Something about Eva. 'Lovely Eva, maddening Eva! I love Eva! Eva! Eva!'"

"Eva? Wasn't it 'Evelyn? Poor Evelyn?'"

"No, it was Eva. I thought he might mean the girl I had just seen carried out. It was an unpleasant experience, hearing this bird shriek out these cries in the face of the man lying dead at my feet."

"Miss Butterworth, you didn't simply stand over that man. You knelt down and looked in his face."

"I acknowledge it, and caught my dress in the filagree of the cross. Naturally I would not stand stock still with a man drawing his last breath under my eye."

"And what else did you do? You went to the table——"

"Yes, I went to the table."

"And moved the inkstand?"

"Yes, I moved the inkstand, but very carefully, sir, very carefully."

"Not so carefully but that I could see where it had been sitting before you took it up: the square made by its base in the dust of the table did not coincide with the place afterwards occupied by it."

"Ah, that comes from your having on your glasses and I not. I endeavored to set it down in the precise place from which I lifted it."

"Why did you take it up at all? What were you looking for?"

"For clews, Mr. Gryce. You must forgive me, but I was seeking for clews. I moved several things. I was hunting for the line of writing which ought to explain this murder."

"The line of writing?"

"Yes. I have not told you what the young girl said as she slipped with her companion into the crowd."

"No; you have spoken of no words. Have you any such clew as that? Miss Butterworth, you are fortunate, very fortunate."

Mr. Gryce's look and gesture were eloquent, but Miss Butterworth, with an access of dignity, quietly remarked:

"I was not to blame for being in the way when they passed, nor could I help hearing what she said."

"And what was it, madam? Did she mention a paper?"

"Yes, she cried in what I now remember to have been a tone of affright: 'You have left that line of writing behind!' I did not attach much importance to these words then, but when I came upon the dying man, so evidently the victim of murder, I recalled what his late visitor had said and looked about for this piece of writing."

"And did you find it, Miss Butterworth? I am ready, as you see, for any revelation you may now make."

"For one which would reflect dishonor on me? If I had found any paper explaining this tragedy, I should have felt bound to have called the attention of the police to it. I did notify them of the crime itself."

"Yes, madam; and we are obliged to you; but how about your silence in regard to the fact of two persons having left that house immediately upon, or just preceding, the death of its master?"

"I reserved that bit of information. I waited to see if the police would not get wind of these people without my help. I sincerely wished to keep my name out of this inquiry. Yet I feel a decided relief now that I have made my confession. I never could have rested properly after seeing so much, and——"

"Well?"

"Thinking my own thoughts in regard to what I saw, if I had found myself compelled to bridle my tongue while false scents were being followed and delicate clews overlooked or discarded without proper attention. I regard this murder as offering the most difficult problem that has ever come in my way, and, therefore——"

"Yes, madam."

"I cannot but wonder if an opportunity has been afforded me for retrieving myself in your eyes. I do not care for the opinion of any one else as to my ability or discretion; but I should like to make you forget my last despicable failure in Lost Man's Lane. It is a sore remembrance to me, Mr. Gryce, which nothing but a fresh success can make me forget."

"Madam, I understand you. You have formulated some theory. You consider the young man with the tell-tale face guilty of Mr. Adams's death. Well, it is very possible. I never thought the butler was rehearsing a crime he had himself committed."

"Do you know who the young man is I saw leaving that house so hurriedly?"

"Not the least in the world. You are the first to bring him to my attention."

"And the young girl with the blonde hair?"

"It is the first I have heard of her, too."

"I did not scatter the rose leaves that were found on that floor."

"No, it was she. She probably wore a bouquet in her belt."

"Nor was that frippery parasol mine, though I did lose a good, stout, serviceable one somewhere that day."

"It was hers; I have no doubt of it."

"Left by her in the little room where she was whiling away the time during which the gentlemen conversed together, possibly about that bit of writing she afterward alluded to."

"Certainly."

"Her mind was not expectant of evil, for she was smoothing her hair when the shock came——"

"Yes, madam, I follow you."

"And had to be carried out of the place after——"

"What?"

"She had placed that cross on Mr. Adams's breast. That was a woman's act, Mr. Gryce."

"I am glad to hear you say so. The placing of that cross on a layman's breast was a mystery to me, and is still, I must own. Great remorse or great fright only can account for it."

"You will find many mysteries in this case, Mr. Gryce."

"As great a number as I ever encountered."

"I have to add one."

"Another?"

"It concerns the old butler."

"I thought you did not see him."

"I did not see him in the room where Mr. Adams lay."

"Ah! Where, then?"

"Upstairs. My interest was not confined to the scene of the murder. Wishing to spread the alarm, and not being able to rouse any one below, I crept upstairs, and so came upon this poor wretch going through the significant pantomime that has been so vividly described in the papers."

"Ah! Unpleasant for you, very. I imagine you did not stop to talk to him."

"No, I fled. I was extremely shaken up by this time and knew only one thing to do, and that was to escape. But I carried one as yet unsolved enigma with me. How came I to hear this man's cries in

Mr. Adams's study, and yet find him on the second floor when I came to search the house? He had not time to mount the stairs while I was passing down the hall."

"It is a case of mistaken impression. Your ears played you false. The cries came from above, not from Mr. Adams's study."

"My ears are not accustomed to play me tricks. You must seek another explanation."

"I have ransacked the house; there are no back stairs."

"If there were, the study does not communicate with them."

"And you heard his voice in the study?"

"Plainly."

"Well, you have given me a poser, madam."

"And I will give you another. If he was the perpetrator of this crime, how comes it that he was not detected and denounced by the young people I saw going out? If, on the contrary, he was simply the witness of another man's blow—a blow which horrified him so much that it unseated his reason—how comes it that he was able to slide away from the door where he must have stood without attracting the attention and bringing down upon himself the vengeance of the guilty murderer?"

"He may be one of the noiseless kind, or, rather, may have been such before this shock unsettled his mind."

"True, but he would have been seen. Recall the position of the doorway. If Mr. Adams fell where he was struck, the assailant must have had that door directly before him. He could not have helped seeing any one standing in it."

"That is true; your observations are quite correct. But those young people were in a disordered state of mind. The condition in which they issued from the house proves this. They probably did not trouble themselves about this man. Escape was all they sought. And, you see, they did escape."

"But you will find them. A man who can locate a woman in this great city of ours with no other clew than five spangles, dropped from her gown, will certainly make this parasol tell the name of its owner."

"Ah, madam, the credit of this feat is not due to me. It was the initial stroke of a young man I propose to adopt into my home and heart; the same who brought you here to-night. Not much to look at, madam, but promising, very promising. But I doubt if even he can discover the young lady you mean, with no other aid than is given by this parasol. New York is a big place, ma'am, a big place. Do you know how Sweetwater came to find you? Through your virtues, ma'am; through your neat and methodical habits. Had you been of a careless turn of mind and not given to mending your dresses when you tore them, he might have worn his heart out in a vain search for the lady who had dropped the five spangles in Mr. Adams's study. Now luck, or, rather, your own commendable habit, was in his favor this time; but in the prospective search you mentioned, he will probably have no such assistance."

"Nor will he need it. I have unbounded faith in your genius, which, after all, is back of the skilfulness of this new pupil of yours. You will discover by some means the lady with the dove-colored plumes, and through her the young gentleman who accompanied her."

"We shall at least put our energies to work in that direction. Sweetwater may have an idea——"

"And I may have one."

"You?"

"Yes; I indulged in but little sleep last night. That dreadful room with its unsolved mystery was ever before me. Thoughts would come; possibilities would suggest themselves. I imagined myself probing its secrets to the bottom and——"

"Wait, madam; how many of its so-called secrets do you know? You said nothing about the lantern."

"It was burning with a red light when I entered."

"You did not touch the buttons arranged along the table top?"

"No; if there is one thing I do not touch, it is anything which suggests an electrical contrivance. I am intensely feminine, sir, in all my instincts, and mechanisms of any kind alarm me. To all such things I give a wide berth. I have not even a telephone in my house. Some allowance must be made for the natural timidity of woman."

Mr. Gryce suppressed a smile. "It is a pity," he remarked. "Had you brought another light upon the scene, you might have been blessed with an idea on a subject that is as puzzling as any connected with the whole affair."

"You have not heard what I have to say on a still more important matter," said she. "When we have exhausted the one topic, we may both feel like turning on the fresh lights you speak of. Mr. Gryce, on what does this mystery hinge? On the bit of writing which these young people were so alarmed at having left behind them."

"Ah! It is from that you would work! Well, it is a good point to start from. But we have found no such bit of writing."

"Have you searched for it? You did not know till now that any importance might be attached to a morsel of paper with some half-dozen words written on it."

"True, but a detective searches just the same. We ransacked that room as few rooms have been ransacked in years. Not for a known clew, but for an unknown one. It seemed necessary in the first place to learn who this man was. His papers were consequently examined. But they told nothing. If there had been a scrap of writing within view or in his desk——"

"It was not on his person? You had his pockets searched, his clothes——"

"A man who has died from violence is always searched, madam. I leave no stone unturned in a mysterious case like this."

Miss Butterworth's face assumed an indefinable expression of satisfaction, which did not escape Mr. Gryce's eye, though that member was fixed, according to his old habit, on the miniature of her father which she wore, in defiance of fashion, at her throat.

"I wonder," said she, in a musing tone, "if I imagined or really saw on Mr. Adams's face a most extraordinary expression; something more than the surprise or anguish following a mortal blow? A look of determination, arguing some superhuman resolve taken at the moment of death, or—can you read that face for me? Or did you fail to perceive aught of what I say? It would really be an aid to me at this moment to know."

"I noted that look. It was not a common one. But I cannot read it for you——"

"I wonder if the young man you call Sweetwater can. I certainly think it has a decided bearing on this mystery; such a fold to the lips, such a look of mingled grief and—what was that you said? Sweetwater has not been admitted to the room of death? Well, well, I shall have to make my own suggestion, then. I shall have to part with an idea that may be totally valueless, but which has impressed me so that it must out, if I am to have any peace to-night. Mr. Gryce, allow me to whisper in your ear. Some things lose force when spoken aloud."

And leaning forward, she breathed a short sentence into his ear which made him start and regard her with an amazement which rapidly grew into admiration.

"Madam!" he cried, rising up that he might the better honor her with one of his low bows, "your idea, whether valueless or not, is one which is worthy of the acute lady who proffers it. We will act on it, ma'am, act at once. Wait till I have given my orders. I will not keep you long."

And with another bow, he left the room.

CHAPTER VII

AMOS'S SON

Miss Butterworth had been brought up in a strict school of manners. When she sat, she sat still; when she moved, she moved quickly, firmly, but with no unnecessary disturbance. Fidgets were unknown to her. Yet when she found herself alone after this interview, it was with difficulty she could restrain herself from indulging in some of those outward manifestations of uneasiness which she had all her life reprobated in the more nervous members of her own sex. She was anxious, and she showed it, like the sensible woman she was, and was glad enough when Mr. Gryce finally returned and, accosting her with a smile, said almost gayly:

"Well, that is seen to! And all we have to do now is to await the result. Madam, have you any further ideas? If so, I should be glad to have the benefit of them."

Her self-possession was at once restored.

"You would?" she repeated, eying him somewhat doubtfully. "I should like to be assured of the value of the one I have already advanced, before I venture upon another. Let us enter into a conference instead; compare notes; tell, for instance, why neither of us look on Bartow as the guilty man."

"I thought we had exhausted that topic. Your suspicions were aroused by the young couple you saw leaving the house, while mine—well, madam, to you, at least, I may admit that there is something in the mute's gestures and general manner which conveys to my mind the impression that he is engaged in rehearsing something he has seen, rather than something he has done; and as yet I have seen no reason for doubting the truth of this impression."

"I was affected in the same way, and would have been, even if I had not already had my suspicions turned in another direction.

Besides, it is more natural for a man to be driven insane by another's act than by his own."

"Yes, if he loved the victim."

"And did not Bartow?"

"He does not mourn Mr. Adams."

"But he is no longer master of his emotions."

"Very true; but if we take any of his actions as a clew to the situation, we must take all. We believe from his gestures that he is giving us a literal copy of acts he has seen performed. Then, why pass over the gleam of infernal joy that lights his face after the whole is over? It is as if he rejoiced over the deed, or at least found immeasurable satisfaction in it."

"Perhaps it is still a copy of what he saw; the murderer may have rejoiced. But no, there was no joy in the face of the young man I saw rushing away from this scene of violence. Quite the contrary. Mr. Gryce, we are in deep waters. I feel myself wellnigh submerged by them."

"Hold up your head, madam. Every flood has its ebb. If you allow yourself to go under, what will become of me?"

"You are disposed to humor, Mr. Gryce. It is a good sign. You are never humorous when perplexed. Somewhere you must see daylight."

"Let us proceed with our argument. Illumination frequently comes from the most unexpected quarter."

"Very well, then, let us put the old man's joy down as one of the mysteries to be explained later. Have you thought of him as a possible accomplice?"

"Certainly; but this supposition is open to the same objection as that which made him the motive power in this murder. One is not driven insane by an expected horror. It takes shock to unsettle the brain. He was not looking for the death of his master."

"True. We may consider that matter as settled. Bartow was an innocent witness of this crime, and, having nothing to fear, may be trusted to reproduce in his pantomimic action its exact features."

"Very good. Continue, madam. Nothing but profit is likely to follow an argument presented by Miss Butterworth."

The old detective's tone was serious, his manner perfect; but Miss Butterworth, ever on the look-out for sarcasm from his lips, bridled a little, though in no other way did she show her displeasure.

"Let us, then, recall his precise gestures, remembering that he must have surprised the assailant from the study doorway, and so have seen the assault from over his master's shoulder."

"In other words, directly in front of him. Now what was his first move?"

"His first move, as now seen, is to raise his right arm and stretch it behind him, while he leans forward for the imaginary dagger. What does that mean?"

"I should find it hard to say. But I did not see him do that. When I came upon him, he was thrusting with his left hand across his own body—a vicious thrust and with his left hand. That is a point, Mr. Gryce."

"Yes, especially as the doctors agree that Mr. Adams was killed by a left-handed blow."

"You don't say! Don't you see the difficulty, then?"

"The difficulty, madam?"

"Bartow was standing face to face with the assailant. In imitating him, especially in his unreasoning state of mind, he would lift the arm opposite to the one whose action he mimics, which, in this case, would be the assailant's right. Try, for the moment, to mimic my actions. See! I lift this hand, and instinctively (nay, I detected the movement, sir, quickly as you remembered yourself), you raise the one directly opposite to it. It is like seeing yourself in a mirror. You turn your head to the right, but your image turns to the left."

Mr. Gryce's laugh rang out in spite of himself. He was not often caught napping, but this woman exercised a species of fascination upon him at times, and it rather amused than offended him, when he was obliged to acknowledge himself defeated.

"Very good! You have proved your point quite satisfactorily; but what conclusions are to be drawn from it? That the man was not left-handed, or that he was not standing in the place you have assigned to him?"

"Shall we go against the doctors? They say that the blow was a left-handed one. Mr. Gryce, I would give anything for an hour spent with you in Mr. Adams's study, with Bartow free to move about at his will. I think we would learn more by watching him for a short space of time than in talking as we are doing for an hour."

It was said tentatively, almost timidly. Miss Butterworth had some sense of the temerity involved in this suggestion even if, according to her own declaration, she had no curiosity. "I don't want to be disagreeable," she smiled.

She was so far from being so that Mr. Gryce was taken unawares, and for once in his life became impulsive.

"I think it can be managed, madam; that is, after the funeral. There are too many officials now in the house, and——"

"Of course, of course," she acceded. "I should not think of obtruding myself at present. But the case is so interesting, and my connection with it so peculiar, that I sometimes forget myself. Do you think"—here she became quite nervous for one of her marked self-control—"that I have laid myself open to a summons from the coroner?"

Mr. Gryce grew thoughtful, eyed the good lady, or rather her folded hands, with an air of some compassion, and finally replied:

"The facts regarding this affair come in so slowly that I doubt if the inquest is held for several days. Meanwhile we may light on those two young people ourselves. If so, the coroner may *overlook* your share in bringing them to our notice."

There was a sly emphasis on the word, and a subtle humor in his look that showed the old detective at his worst. But Miss Butterworth did not resent it; she was too full of a fresh confession she had to make.

"Ah," said she, "if they had been the only persons I encountered there. But they were not. Another person entered the house before I left it, and I may be obliged to speak of him."

"Of him? Really, madam, you are a mine of intelligence."

"Yes, sir," was the meek reply; meek, when you consider from whose lips it came. "I ought to have spoken of him before, but I never like to mix matters, and this old gentleman——"

"Old gentleman!"

"Yes, sir, very old and very much of a gentleman, did not appear to have any connection with the crime beyond knowing the murdered man."

"Ah, but that's a big connection, ma'am. To find some one who knew Mr. Adams—really, madam, patience has its limits, and I must press you to speak."

"Oh, I will speak! The time has come for it. Besides, I'm quite ready to discuss this new theme; it is very interesting."

"Suppose we begin, then, by a detailed account of your adventures in this house of death," dryly suggested the detective. "Your full adventures, madam, with nothing left out."

"I appreciate the sarcasm, but nothing has been left out except what I am about to relate to you. It happened just as I was leaving the house."

"What did? I hate to ask you to be more explicit. But, in the interests of justice——"

"You are quite right. As I was going out, then, I encountered an elderly gentleman coming in. His hand had just touched the bell handle. You will acknowledge that it was a perplexing moment for me. His face, which was well preserved for his years, wore an air of expectation that was almost gay. He glanced in astonishment at mine, which, whatever its usual serenity, certainly must have borne marks of deep emotion. Neither of us spoke. At last he inquired politely if he might enter, and said something about having an appointment with some one in the study. At which I stepped briskly enough aside, I assure you, for this might mean—What did you say? Did I close the door? I assuredly did. Was I to let the whole of —— Street into the horrors of this house at a moment when a poor old man—No, I didn't go out myself. Why should I? Was I to leave a man on the verge of eighty—excuse me, not every man of eighty is so hale and vigorous as yourself—to enter such a scene alone? Besides, I had not warned him of the condition of the only other living occupant of the house."

"Discreet, very. Quite what was to be expected of you, Miss Butterworth. More than that. You followed him, no doubt, with careful supervision, down the hall."

"Most certainly! What would you have thought of me if I had not? He was in a strange house; there was no servant to guide him, he wanted to know the way to the study, and I politely showed him there."

"Kind of you, madam,—very. It must have been an interesting moment to you."

"Very interesting! Too interesting! I own that I am not made entirely of steel, sir, and the shock he received at finding a dead man awaiting him, instead of a live one, was more or less communicated to me. Yet I stood my ground."

"Admirable! I could have done no better myself. And so this man who had an appointment with Mr. Adams was shocked, really shocked, at finding him lying there under a cross, dead?"

"Yes, there was no doubting that. Shocked, surprised, terrified, and something more. It is that something more which has proved my perplexity. I cannot make it out, not even in thinking it over. Was it the fascination which all horrible sights exert on the morbid, or was it a sudden realization of some danger he had escaped, or of some difficulty yet awaiting him? Hard to say, Mr. Gryce, hard to say; but you may take my word for it that there was more to him in this meeting than an unexpected stumbling upon a dead man where he expected to find a live one. Yet he made no sound after that first cry, and hardly any movement. He just stared at the figure on the floor; then at his face, which he seemed to devour, at first with curiosity, then with hate, then with terror, and lastly—how can I express myself?—with a sort of hellish humor that in another moment might have broken into something like a laugh, if the bird, which I had failed to observe up to this moment, had not waked in its high cage, and, thrusting its beak between the bars, shrilled out in the most alarming of tones: 'Remember Evelyn!' That startled the old man even more than the sight on the floor had done. He turned round, and I saw his fist rise as if against some menacing intruder, but it quickly fell again as his eyes encountered the picture which hung before him, and with a cringe painful to see in one of his years, he sidled back till he reached the doorway. Here he paused a minute to give another look at the man outstretched at his feet, and I heard him say:

"'It is Amos's son, not Amos! Is it fatality, or did he plan this meeting, thinking——'

"But here he caught sight of my figure in the antechamber beyond, and resuming in an instant his former debonair manner, he bowed very low and opened his lips as if about to ask a question. But he evidently thought better of it, for he strode by me and made his way to the front door without a word. Being an intruder myself, I did not like to stop him. But I am sorry now for the consideration I showed him; for just before he stepped out, his emotion—the special character of which, I own to you, I find impossible to understand—culminated in a burst of raucous laughter which added the final horror to this amazing adventure. Then he went out, and in the last glimpse I had of him before the door shut he wore the same look of easy self-satisfaction with which he had entered this place of death some fifteen minutes before."

"Remarkable! Some secret history there! That man must be found. He can throw light upon Mr. Adams's past. 'Amos's son,' he called him? Who is Amos? Mr. Adams's name was Felix. Felix, the son of Amos. Perhaps this connection of names may lead to something. It is not a common one, and if given to the papers, may result in our receiving a clew to a mystery which seems impenetrable. Your stay in Mr. Adams's house was quite productive, ma'am. Did you prolong it after the departure of this old man?"

"No, sir, I had had my fill of the mysterious, and left immediately after him. Ashamed of the spirit of investigation which had led me to enter the house, I made a street boy the medium of my communication to the police, and would have been glad if I could have so escaped all responsibility in the matter. But the irony of fate follows me as it does others. A clew was left of my presence, which involves me in this affair, whether I will or no. Was the hand of Providence in this? Perhaps. The future will tell. And now, Mr. Gryce, since my budget is quite empty and the hour late, I will take my leave. If you hear from that bit of paper——"

"If I hear from it in the way you suggest I will let you know. It will be the least I can do for a lady who has done so much for me."

"Now you flatter me—proof positive that I have stayed a minute longer than was judicious. Good evening, Mr. Gryce. What? I have not stayed too long? You have something else to ask."

"Yes, and this time it is concerning a matter personal to yourself. May I inquire if you wore the same bonnet yesterday that you do to-day?"

"No, sir. I know you have a good reason for this question, and so will not express my surprise. Yesterday I was in reception costume, and my bonnet was a jet one——"

"With long strings tied under the chin?"

"No, sir, short strings; long strings are no longer the fashion."

"But you wore something which fell from your neck?"

"Yes, a boa—a feather boa. How came you to know it, sir? Did I leave my image in one of the mirrors?"

"Hardly. If so, I should not have expected it to speak. You merely wrote the fact on the study table top. Or so I have dared to think. You or the young lady—did she wear ribbons or streamers, too?"

"That I cannot say. Her face was all I saw, and the skirt of a dove-colored silk dress."

"Then you must settle the question for me in this way. If on the tips of that boa of yours you find the faintest evidence of its having been dipped in blood, I shall know that the streaks found on the top of the table I speak of were evidences of your presence there. But if your boa is clean, or was not long enough to touch that dying man as you leaned over him, then we have proof that the young lady with the dove-colored plumes fingered that table also, instead of falling at once into the condition in which you saw her carried out."

"I fear that it is my boa which will tell the tale: another proof of the fallibility of man, or, rather, woman. In secret search for clews I left behind me traces of my own presence. I really feel mortified, sir, and you have quite the advantage of me."

And with this show of humility, which may not have been entirely sincere, this estimable lady took her departure.

Did Mr. Gryce suffer from any qualms of conscience at having elicited so much and imparted so little? I doubt it. Mr. Gryce's conscience was quite seared in certain places.

CHAPTER VIII

IN THE ROUND OF THE STAIRCASE

The next morning Mr. Gryce received a small communication from Miss Butterworth at or near the very time she received one from him. Hers ran:

You were quite correct. So far as appears, I was the only person to lean over Mr. Adams's study table after his unfortunate death. I have had to clip the ends of my boa.

His was equally laconic:

My compliments, madam! Mr. Adams's jaws have been forced apart. A small piece of paper was found clinched between his teeth. This paper has been recovered, and will be read at the inquest. Perhaps a few favored persons may be granted the opportunity of reading it before then, notably yourself.

Of the two letters the latter naturally occasioned the greater excitement in the recipient. The complacency of Miss Butterworth was superb, and being the result of something that could not be communicated to those about her, occasioned in the household much speculation as to its cause.

At Police Headquarters more than one man was kept busy listening to the idle tales of a crowd of would-be informers. The results which had failed to follow the first day's publication of the crime came rapidly in during the second. There were innumerable persons of all ages and conditions who were ready to tell how they had seen this and that one issue from Mr. Adams's house on the afternoon of his death, but when asked to give a description of these persons, lost themselves in generalities as tedious as they were unprofitable. One garrulous old woman had observed a lady of genteel appearance open the door to an elderly gentleman in a great-coat; and a fashionably dressed young woman came in all breathless to relate how a young man with a very pale young lady on his arm ran against her as she was going by this house at the very hour Mr. Adams was said to have been murdered. She could not be sure of knowing the young man again, and could not say if the young lady was blonde or brunette, only that she was awfully pale and had a beautiful gray feather in her hat.

Others were ready with similar stories, which confirmed, without adding to, the facts already known, and night came on without much progress having been made toward the unravelling of this formidable mystery.

On the next day Mr. Adams's funeral took place. No relatives or intimate friends having come forward, his landlord attended to these rites and his banker acted the part of chief mourner. As his body was carried out of the house, a half-dozen detectives mingled with the crowd blocking the thoroughfare in front, but nothing came of their surveillance here or at the cemetery to which the remains were speedily carried. The problem which had been presented to the police had to be worked out from such material as had already come to hand; and, in forcible recognition of this fact, Mr. Gryce excused himself one evening at Headquarters and proceeded quite alone and on foot to the dark and apparently closed house in which the tragedy had occurred.

He entered with a key, and once inside, proceeded to light up the whole house. This done, he took a look at the study, saw that the cross had been replaced on the wall, the bird-cage rehung on its hook under the ceiling, and everything put in its wonted order, with the exception of the broken casings, which still yawned in a state of disrepair on either side of the doorway leading into the study. The steel plate had been shoved back into the place prepared for it by Mr. Adams, but the glimpses still to be seen of its blue surface through the hole made in the wall of the antechamber formed anything but an attractive feature in the scene, and Mr. Gryce, with something of the instinct and much of the deftness of a housewife, proceeded to pull up a couple of rugs from the parlor floor and string them over these openings. Then he consulted his watch, and finding that it was within an hour of nine o'clock, took up his stand behind the curtains of the parlor window. Soon, for the person expected was as prompt as himself, he saw a carriage stop and a lady alight, and he hastened to the front door to receive her. It was Miss Butterworth.

"Madam, your punctuality is equal to my own," said he. "Have you ordered your coachman to drive away?"

"Only as far as the corner," she returned, as she followed him down the hall. "There he will await the call of your whistle."

"Nothing could be better. Are you afraid to remain for a moment alone, while I watch from the window the arrival of the other persons we expect? At present there is no one in the house but ourselves."

"If I was subject to fear in a matter of this kind, I should not be here at all. Besides, the house is very cheerfully lighted. I see you have chosen a crimson light for illuminating the study."

"Because a crimson light was burning when Mr. Adams died."

"Remember Evelyn!" called out a voice.

"Oh, you have brought back the bird!" exclaimed Miss Butterworth. "That is not the cry with which it greeted me before. It was 'Eva! Lovely Eva!' Do you suppose Eva and Evelyn are the same?"

"Madam, we have so many riddles before us that we will let this one go for the present. I expect Mr. Adams's valet here in a moment."

"Sir, you relieve me of an immense weight. I was afraid that the privilege of being present at the test you propose to make was not to be accorded me."

"Miss Butterworth, you have earned a seat at this experiment. Bartow has been given a key, and will enter as of old in entire freedom to do as he wills. We have simply to watch his movements."

"In this room, sir? I do not think I shall like that. I had rather not meet this madman face to face."

"You will not be called upon to do so. We do not wish him to be startled by encountering any watchful eye. Irresponsible as he is, he must be allowed to move about without anything to distract his attention. Nothing must stand in the way of his following those impulses which may yield us a clew to his habits and the ways of this peculiar household. I propose to place you where the chances are least in favor of your being seen by him—in this parlor, madam, which we have every reason to believe was seldom opened during Mr. Adams's lifetime."

"You must put out the gas, then, or the unaccustomed light will attract his attention."

"I will not only put out the gas, but I will draw the portières close, making this little hole for your eye and this one for mine. A common expedient, madam; but serviceable, madam, serviceable."

The snort which Miss Butterworth gave as she thus found herself drawn up in darkness before a curtain, in company with this plausible old man, but feebly conveyed her sensations, which were naturally complex and a little puzzling to herself. Had she been the possessor of a lively curiosity (but we know from her own lips that she was not), she might have found some enjoyment in the situation. But being where she was solely from a sense of duty, she probably blushed behind her screen at the position in which she found herself, in the cause of truth and justice; or would have done so if the opening of the front door at that moment had not told her that the critical moment had arrived and that the deaf-and-dumb valet had just been introduced into the house.

The faintest "Hush!" from Mr. Gryce warned her that her surmise was correct, and, bending her every energy to listen, she watched for the expected appearance of this man in the antechamber of Mr. Adams's former study.

He came even sooner than she was prepared to see him, and laying down his hat on a table near the doorway, advanced with a busy air toward the portière he had doubtless been in the habit of lifting twenty times a day. But he barely touched it this time. Something seen, or unseen, prevented him from entering. Was it the memory of what he had last beheld there? Or had he noticed the rugs hanging in an unaccustomed way on either side of the damaged casings? Neither, apparently, for he simply turned away with a meek look, wholly mechanical, and taking up his hat again, left the antechamber and proceeded softly upstairs.

"I will follow him," whispered Mr. Gryce. "Don't be afraid, ma'am. This whistle will bring a man in from the street at once."

"I am not afraid. I would be ashamed——"

But it was useless for her to finish this disclaimer. Mr. Gryce was already in the hall. He returned speedily, and saying that the experiment was likely to be a failure, as the old man had gone to his own room and was preparing himself for bed, he led the way into the study, and with purpose, or without a purpose—who knows?—idly touched a button on the table top, thus throwing a new light on the scene. It was Miss Butterworth's first experience of this change of light, and she was observing the effect made by the violet glow now thrown over the picture and the other rich articles in the room when her admiration was cut short, and Mr. Gryce's half-uttered remark also, by the faint sound of the valet's descending steps.

Indeed, they had barely time to regain their old position behind the parlor portières when Bartow was seen hurrying in from the hall with his former busy air, which this time remained unchecked.

Crossing to his master's study, he paused for an infinitesimal length of time on the threshold, as if conscious of something being amiss, then went into the room beyond, and, without a glance in the direction of the rug, which had been carefully relaid on the spot where his master had fallen, began to make such arrangements for the night as he was in the habit of making at this hour. He brought a bottle of wine from the cupboard and set it on the table, and then a glass, which he first wiped scrupulously clean. Then he took out his master's dressing gown and slippers, and, placing them to hand, went into the bedroom.

By this time the two watchers had crept from their concealment near enough to note what he was doing in the bedroom. He was stooping over the comb which Mr. Gryce had left lying on the floor. This small object in such a place seemed to surprise him. He took it up, shook his head, and put it back on the dresser. Then he turned down his master's bed.

"Poor fool!" murmured Miss Butterworth as she and her companion crept back to their old place behind the parlor curtains, "he has forgotten everything but his old routine duties. We shall get nothing from this man."

But she stopped suddenly; they both stopped. Bartow was in the middle of the study, with his eyes fixed on his master's empty chair in an inquiring way that spoke volumes. Then he turned, and gazed earnestly at the rug where he had last seen that master lying outstretched and breathless; and awakening to a realization of what had happened, fell into his most violent self and proceeded to go through the series of actions which they were now bound to consider a reproduction of what he had previously seen take place there. Then he went softly out, and crept away upstairs.

Mr. Gryce and Miss Butterworth stepped at once into the light, and surveyed each other with a look of marked discouragement. Then the latter, with a sudden gleam of enthusiasm, cried quickly:

"Turn on another color, and let us see what will happen. I have an idea it will fetch the old man down again."

Mr. Gryce's brows went up.

"Do you think he can see through the floor?"

But he touched a button, and a rich blue took the place of the violet.

Nothing happened.

Miss Butterworth looked disturbed.

"I have confidence in your theories," began Mr. Gryce, "but when they imply the possibility of this man seeing through blank walls and obeying signals which can have no signification to any one on the floor above——"

"Hark!" she cried, holding up one finger with a triumphant air. The old man's steps could be heard descending.

This time he approached with considerable feebleness, passed slowly into the study, advanced to the table, and reached out his hands as if to lift something which he expected to find there. Seeing nothing, he glanced in astonishment up at the book shelves and then back to the table, shook his head, and suddenly collapsing, sank in a doze on the nearest chair.

Miss Butterworth drew a long breath, eyed Mr. Gryce with some curiosity, and then triumphantly exclaimed:

"Can you read the meaning of all that? I think I can. Don't you see that he came expecting to find a pile of books on the table which it was probably his business to restore to their shelves?"

"But how can he know what light is burning here? You can see for yourself that there is no possible communication between this room and the one in which he has always been found by any one going above."

Miss Butterworth's manner showed a hesitation that was almost naive. She smiled, and there was apology in her smile, though none in her voice, as she remarked with odd breaks:

"When I went upstairs—you know I went upstairs when I was here before—I saw a little thing—a very little thing—which you doubtless observed yourself and which may explain, though I do not know how, why Bartow can perceive these lights from the floor above."

"I shall be very glad to hear about it, madam. I thought I had thoroughly searched those rooms——"

"And the halls?"

"And the halls; and that nothing in them could have escaped my eyes. But if you have a more patient vision than myself——"

"Or make it my business to look lower——"

"How?"

"To look lower; to look on the floor, say."

"On the floor?"

"The floor sometimes reveals much: shows where a person steps the oftenest, and, therefore, where he has the most business. You must have noticed how marred the woodwork is at the edge of the carpeting on that little landing above."

"In the round of the staircase?"

"Yes."

Mr. Gryce did not think it worth his while to answer. Perhaps he had not time; for leaving the valet where he was, and Miss Butterworth where she was (only she would not be left, but followed him), he made his way upstairs, and paused at the place she had mentioned, with a curious look at the floor.

"You see, it has been much trodden here," she said; at which gentle reminder of her presence he gave a start; possibly he had not heard her behind him, and after sixty years of hard service even a detective may be excused a slight nervousness. "Now, why should it be trodden here? There is no apparent reason why any one should shuffle to and fro in this corner. The stair is wide, especially here, and there is no window——"

Mr. Gryce, whose eye had been travelling over the wall, reached over her shoulder to one of the dozen pictures hanging at intervals from the bottom to the top of the staircase, and pulling it away from the wall, on which it hung decidedly askew, revealed a round opening through which poured a ray of blue light which could only proceed from the vault of the adjoining study.

"No window," he repeated. "No, but an opening into the study wall which answers the same purpose. Miss Butterworth, your eye is to be trusted every time. I only wonder you did not pull this picture aside yourself."

"It was not hanging crooked then. Besides I was in a hurry. I had just come from my encounter with this demented man. I had noticed the marks on the landing, and the worn edges of the carpet, on my way upstairs. I was in no condition to observe them on my way down."

"I see."

Miss Butterworth ran her foot to and fro over the flooring they were examining.

"Bartow was evidently in the habit of coming here constantly," said she, "probably to learn whether his master had need of him. Ingenious in Mr. Adams to contrive signals for communication with this man! He certainly had great use for his deaf-and-dumb servant. So one mystery is solved!"

"And if I am not mistaken, we can by a glance through this loophole obtain the answer to another. You are wondering, I believe, how Bartow, if he followed the movements of the assailant from the doorway, came to thrust with his left hand, instead of with his right. Now if he saw the tragedy from this point, he saw it over the assailant's shoulder, instead of face to face. What follows? He would imitate literally the movements of the man he saw, turn in the same direction and strike with the same hand."

"Mr. Gryce, we are beginning to untangle the threads that looked so complicated. Ah, what is that? Why, it's that bird! His cage must be very nearly under this hole."

"A little to one side, madam, but near enough to give you a start. What was it he cried then?"

"Oh, those sympathetic words about Eva! 'Poor Eva!'"

"Well, give a glance to Bartow. You can see him very well from here."

Miss Butterworth put her eye again to the opening, and gave a grunt, a very decided grunt. With her a grunt was significant of surprise.

"He is shaking his fist; he is all alive with passion. He looks as if he would like to kill the bird."

"Perhaps that is why the creature was strung up so high. You may be sure Mr. Adams had some basis for his idiosyncrasies."

"I begin to think so. I don't know that I care to go back where that man is. He has a very murderous look."

"And a very feeble arm, Miss Butterworth. You are safe under my protection. My arm is not feeble."

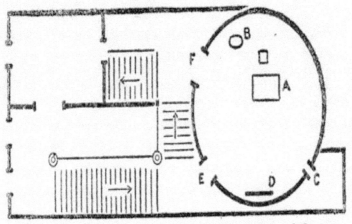

A-TABLE. B-SMALL STAND. C-DOOR TO BEDROOM D-EVELYN'S PICTURE E-LOOPHOLE ON STAIR LANDING. F- ENTRANCE TO STUDY.

[Illustration: A-Table. B-Small Stand. C-Door to Bedroom. D-Evelyn's Picture E-Loophole on Stair Landing. F-Entrance to Study.] [1]

[1] Since my readers may not understand how an opening above the stairway might communicate with Mr. Adams's study, I here submit a diagram of the same. The study walls were very high, forming a rounded extension at the back of the house.

CHAPTER IX

HIGH AND LOW

At the foot of the stairs, Mr. Gryce excused himself, and calling in two or three men whom he had left outside, had the valet removed before taking Miss Butterworth back into the study. When all was quiet again, and they found an opportunity to speak, Mr. Gryce remarked:

"One very important thing has been settled by the experiment we have just made. Bartow is acquitted of participation in this crime."

"Then we can give our full attention to the young people. You have heard nothing from them, I suppose?"

"No."

"Nor from the old man who laughed?"

"No."

Miss Butterworth looked disappointed.

"I thought—it seemed very probable—that the scrap of writing you found would inform you who these were. If it was important enough for the dying man to try to swallow it, it certainly should give some clew to his assailant."

"Unfortunately, it does not do so. It was a veritable scrawl, madam, running something like this: 'I return your daughter to you. She is here. Neither she nor you will ever see me again. Remember Evelyn!' And signed, 'Amos's son.'"

"Amos's son! That is Mr. Adams himself."

"So we have every reason to believe."

"Strange! Unaccountable! And the paper inscribed with these words was found clinched between his teeth! Was the handwriting recognized?"

"Yes, as his own, if we can judge from the specimens we have seen of his signature on the fly-leaves of his books."

"Well, mysteries deepen. And the retaining of this paper was so important to him that even in his death throe he thrust it in this strangest of all hiding-places, as being the only one that could be considered safe from search. And the girl! Her first words on coming to herself were: 'You have left that line of writing behind.' Mr. Gryce, those words, few and inexplicable as they are, contain the key to the whole situation. Will you repeat them again, if you please, sentence by sentence?"

"With pleasure, madam; I have said them often enough to myself. First, then: 'I return your daughter to you!'"

"So! Mr. Adams had some one's daughter in charge whom he returns. Whose daughter? Not that young man's daughter, certainly, for that would necessitate her being a small child. Besides, if these words had been meant for his assailant, why make so remarkable an effort to hide them from him?"

"Very true! I have said the same thing to myself."

"Yet, if not for him, for whom, then? For the old gentleman who came in later?"

"It is possible; since hearing of him I have allowed myself to regard this as among the possibilities, especially as the next words of this strange communication are: 'She is here.' Now the only woman who was there a few minutes previous to this old gentleman's visit was the light-haired girl whom you saw carried out."

"Very true; but why do you reason as if this paper had just been written? It might have been an old scrap, referring to past sorrows or secrets."

"These words were written that afternoon. The paper on which they were scrawled was torn from a sheet of letter paper lying on the desk, and the pen with which they were inscribed—you must have noticed where it lay, quite out of its natural place on the extreme edge of the table."

"Certainly, sir; but I had little idea of the significance we might come to attach to it. These words are connected, then, with the girl I saw. And she is not Evelyn or he would not have repeated in this note the bird's catch-word, 'Remember Evelyn!' I wonder if she is Evelyn?" proceeded Miss Butterworth, pointing to the one large picture which adorned the wall.

"We may call her so for the nonce. So melancholy a face may well suggest some painful family secret. But how explain the violent part played by the young man, who is not mentioned in these abrupt and hastily penned sentences! It is all a mystery, madam, a mystery which we are wasting time to attempt to solve."

"Yet I hate to give it up without an effort. Those words, now. There were some other words you have not repeated to me."

"They came before that injunction, 'Remember Evelyn!' They bespoke a resolve. 'Neither she nor you will ever see me again.'"

"Ah! but these few words are very significant, Mr. Gryce. Could he have dealt that blow himself? May he have been a suicide after all?"

"Madam, you have the right to inquire; but from Bartow's pantomime, you must have perceived it is not a self-inflicted blow he mimics, but a maddened thrust from an outraged hand. Let us keep to our first conclusions; only—to be fair to every possibility—the condition of Mr. Adams's affairs and the absence of all family papers and such documents as may usually be found in a wealthy man's desk prove that he had made some preparation for possible death. It may have come sooner than he expected and in another way, but it was a thought he had indulged in, and— madam, I have a confession to make also. I have not been quite fair to my most valued colleague. The study—that most remarkable of rooms—contains a secret which has not been imparted to you; a very peculiar one, madam, which was revealed to me in a rather startling manner. This room can be, or rather could be, cut off entirely from the rest of the house; made a death-trap of, or rather a tomb, in which this incomprehensible man may have intended to die. Look at this plate of steel. It is worked by a mechanism which forces it across this open doorway. I was behind that plate of steel the other night, and these holes had to be made to let me out."

"Ha! You detectives have your experiences! I should not have enjoyed spending that especial evening with you. But what an old-world tragedy we are unearthing here! I declare"—and the good lady actually rubbed her eyes—"I feel as if transported back to mediæval days. Who says we are living in New York within sound of the cable car and the singing of the telegraph wire?"

"Some men are perfectly capable of bringing the mediæval into Wall Street. I think Mr. Adams was one of those men. Romanticism tinged all his acts, even the death he died. Nor did it cease with his death. It followed him to the tomb. Witness the cross we found lying on his bosom."

"That was the act of another's hand, the result of another's superstition. That shows the presence of a priest or a woman at the moment he died."

"Yet," proceeded Mr. Gryce, with a somewhat wondering air, "he must have had a grain of hard sense in his make-up. All his contrivances worked. He was a mechanical genius, as well as a lover of mystery."

"An odd combination. Strange that we do not feel his spirit infecting the very air of this study. I could almost wish it did. We might then be led to grasp the key to this mystery."

"That," remarked Mr. Gryce, "can be done in only one way. You have already pointed it out. We must trace the young couple who were present at his death struggle. If they cannot be found the case is hopeless."

"And so," said she, "we come around to the point from which we started—proof positive that we are lost in the woods." And Miss Butterworth rose. She felt that for the time being she, at least, had come to the end of her resources.

Mr. Gryce did not seek to detain her. Indeed, he appeared to be anxious to leave the place himself. They, however, stopped long enough to cast one final look around them. As they did so Miss Butterworth's finger slowly rose.

"See!" said she, "you can hardly perceive from this side of the wall the opening made by the removal of that picture on the stair landing. Wouldn't you say that it was in the midst of those folds of dark-colored tapestry up there?"

"Yes, I had already located that spot as the one. With the picture hung up on the other side, it would be quite invisible."

"One needs to keep one's eyes moving in a case like this. That picture must have been drawn aside several times while we were in this room. Yet we failed to notice it."

"That was from not looking high enough. High and low, Mr. Gryce! What goes on at the level of the eye is apparent to every one."

The smile with which he acknowledged this parting shot and prepared to escort her to the door had less of irony than sadness in it. Was he beginning to realize that years tell even on the most sagacious, and that neither high places nor low would have escaped his attention a dozen years before?

CHAPTER X

BRIDE ROSES

"A blonde, you say, sir?"

"Yes, Sweetwater; not of the usual type, but one of those frail, ethereal creatures whom we find it so hard to associate with crime. He, on the contrary, according to Miss Butterworth's description (and her descriptions may be relied upon), is one of those gentlemanly athletes whose towering heads and powerful figures attract universal attention. Seen together, you would be apt to know them. But what reason have we for thinking they will be found together?"

"How were they dressed?"

"Like people of fashion and respectability. He wore a brown-checked suit apparently fresh from the tailor; she, a dove-colored dress with white trimmings. The parasol shows the color of her hat and plumes. Both were young, and (still according to Miss Butterworth) of sensitive temperament and unused to crime; for she was in a fainting condition when carried from the house, and he, with every inducement to self-restraint, showed himself the victim of such powerful emotion that he would have been immediately surrounded and questioned if he had not set his burden down in the vestibule and at once plunged with the girl into the passing crowd. Do you think you can find them, Sweetwater?"

"Have you no clews to their identity beyond this parasol?"

"None, Sweetwater, if you except these few faded rose leaves picked up from the floor of Mr. Adams's study."

"Then you have given me a problem, Mr. Gryce," remarked the young detective dubiously, as he eyed the parasol held out to him and let the rose-leaves drop carelessly through his fingers. "Somehow I do not feel the same assurances of success that I did before. Perhaps I more fully realize the difficulties of any such quest, now that I see how much rests upon chance in these matters. If Miss Butterworth had not been a precise woman, I should have failed in my former attempt, as I am likely to fail in this one. But I will make another effort to locate the owner of this parasol, if only to learn my business by failure. And now, sir, where do you think I am going first? To a florist's, with these faded rose-leaves. Just because every other young fellow on the force would make a start from the parasol, I am going to try and effect one from these rose-leaves. I may be an egotist, but I cannot help that. I can do nothing with the parasol."

"And what do you hope to do with the rose-leaves? How can a florist help you in finding this young woman by means of them?"

"He may be able to say from what kind of a rose they fell, and once I know that, I may succeed in discovering the particular store from which the bouquet was sold to this more or less conspicuous couple."

"You may. I am not the man to throw cold water on any one's schemes. Every man has his own methods, and till they are proved valueless I say nothing."

Young Sweetwater, who was now all nerve, enthusiasm, and hope, bowed. He was satisfied to be allowed to work in his own way.

"I may be back in an hour, and you may not see me for a week," he remarked on leaving.

"Luck to your search!" was the short reply. This ended the interview. In a few minutes more Sweetwater was off.

The hour passed; he did not come back; the day, and still no Sweetwater. Another day went by, enlivened only by an interchange of notes between Mr. Gryce and Miss Butterworth. Hers was read by the old detective with a smile. Perhaps because it was so terse; perhaps because it was so characteristic.

Dear Mr. Gryce:

I do not presume to dictate or even to offer a suggestion to the New York police, but have you inquired of the postman in a certain district whether he can recall the postmark on any of the letters he delivered to Mr. Adams?

A. B.

His, on the contrary, was perused with a frown by his exacting colleague in Gramercy Park. The reason is obvious.

Dear Miss Butterworth:

Suggestions are always in order, and even dictation can be endured from you. The postman delivers too many letters on that block to concern himself with postmarks. Sorry to close another thoroughfare.

E. G.

Meanwhile, the anxiety of both was great; that of Mr. Gryce excessive. He was consequently much relieved when, on the third morning, he found Sweetwater awaiting him at the office, with a satisfied smile lighting up his plain features. He had reserved his story for his special patron, and as soon as they were closeted together he turned with beaming eyes toward the old detective, crying:

"News, sir; good news! I have found them; I have found them both, and by such a happy stroke! It was a blind trail, but when the florist said that those petals might have fallen from a bride rose— well, sir, I know that any woman can carry bride roses, but when I remembered that the clothes of her companion looked as though they had just come from the tailor's, and that she wore gray and white—why, it gave me an idea, and I began my search after this unknown pair at the Bureau of Vital Statistics."

"Brilliant!" ejaculated the old detective. "That is, if the thing worked."

"And it did, sir; it did. I may have been born under a lucky star, probably was, but once started on this line of search, I went straight to the end. Shall I tell you how? Hunting through the list of such persons as had been married within the city limits during the last two weeks, I came upon the name of one Eva Poindexter. Eva! that was a name well-known in the house on —— Street. I decided to follow up this Eva."

"A wise conclusion! And how did you set about it?"

"Why, I went directly to the clergyman who had performed the ceremony. He was a kind and affable dominie, sir, and I had no trouble in talking to him."

"And you described the bride?"

"No, I led the conversation so that he described her."

"Good; and what kind of a woman did he make her out to be? Delicate? Pale?"

"Sir, he had not read the service for so lovely a bride in years. Very slight, almost fragile, but beautiful, and with a delicate bloom which showed her to be in better health than one would judge from her dainty figure. It was a private wedding, sir, celebrated in a hotel parlor; but her father was with her——"

"Her father?" Mr. Gryce's theory received its first shock. Then the old man who had laughed on leaving Mr. Adams's house was not the father to whom those few lines in Mr. Adams's handwriting were addressed. Or this young woman was not the person referred to in those lines.

"Is there anything wrong about that?" inquired Sweetwater.

Mr. Gryce became impassive again.

"No; I had not expected his attendance at the wedding; that is all."

"Sorry, sir, but there is no doubt about his having been there. The bridegroom——"

"Yes, tell me about the bridegroom."

"Was the very man you described to me as leaving Mr. Adams's house with her. Tall, finely developed, with a grand air and gentlemanly manners. Even his clothes correspond with what you told me to expect: a checked suit, brown in color, and of the latest cut. Oh, he is the man!"

Mr. Gryce, with a suddenly developed interest in the lid of his inkstand, recalled the lines which Mr. Adams had written immediately before his death, and found himself wholly at sea. How reconcile facts so diametrically opposed? What allusion could there be in these lines to the new-made bride of another man? They read, rather, as if she were his own bride, as witness:

I return your daughter to you. She is here. Neither she nor you will ever see me again. Remember Evelyn!

AMOS'S SON.

There must be something wrong. Sweetwater must have been led astray by a series of extraordinary coincidences. Dropping the lid of the inkstand in a way to make the young man smile, he looked up.

"I'm afraid it's been a fool chase, Sweetwater. The facts you relate in regard to this couple, the fact of their having been married at all, tally so little with what we have been led to expect from certain other evidences which have come in———"

"Pardon me, sir, but will you hear me out? At the Imperial, where they were married, I learned that the father and daughter had registered as coming from a small place in Pennsylvania; but I could learn nothing in regard to the bridegroom. He had not appeared on the scene till the time for the ceremony, and after the marriage was seen to take his bride away in one carriage while the old gentleman departed in another. The latter concerned me little; it was the young couple I had been detailed to find. Employing the usual means of search, I tracked them to the Waldorf, where I learned what makes it certain that I have been following the right couple. On the afternoon of the very day of Mr. Adams's death, this young husband and wife left the hotel on foot and did not come back. Their clothes, which had all been left behind, were taken away two days later by an elderly gentleman who said he was her father and whose appearance coincides with that of the person registering as such at the Imperial. All of which looks favorable to my theory, does it not, especially when you remember that the bridegroom's name———"

"You have not told it."

"Is Adams, Thomas Adams. Same family as the murdered man, you see. At least, he has the same name."

Mr. Gryce surveyed the young man with admiration, but was not yet disposed to yield him entire credence.

"Humph! I do not wonder you thought it worth your while to follow up the pair, if one of them is named Adams and the other

Eva. But, Sweetwater, the longer you serve on the force the more you will learn that coincidences as strange and unexpected as these do occur at times, and must be taken into account in the elucidation of a difficult problem. Much as I may regret to throw cold water on your hopes, there are reasons for believing that the young man and woman whom we are seeking are not the ones you have busied yourself about for the last two days. Certain facts which have come to light would seem to show that if she had a husband at all, his name would not be Thomas Adams, but Felix, and as the facts I have to bring forward are most direct and unimpeachable, I fear you will have to start again, and on a new tack."

But Sweetwater remained unshaken, and eyed his superior with a vague smile playing about his lips.

"You have not asked me, sir, where I have spent all the time which has elapsed since I saw you last. The investigations I have mentioned did not absorb more than a day."

"Very true. Where have you been, Sweetwater?"

"To Montgomery, sir, to that small town in Pennsylvania from which Mr. Poindexter and his daughter registered."

"Ah, I see! And what did you learn there? Something directly to the point?"

"I learned this, that John Poindexter, father of Eva, had for a friend in early life one Amos Cadwalader."

"Amos!" repeated Mr. Gryce, with an odd look.

"Yes, and that this Amos had a son, Felix."

"Ah!"

"You see, sir, we must be on the right track; coincidences cannot extend through half a dozen names."

"You are right. It is I who have made a mistake in drawing my conclusions too readily. Let us hear about this Amos. You gathered something of his history, no doubt."

"All that was possible, sir. It is closely woven in with that of Poindexter, and presents one feature which may occasion you no surprise, but which, I own, came near nonplussing me. Though the father of Felix, his name was not Adams. I say was not, for he has been dead six months. It was Cadwalader. And Felix went by the name of Cadwalader, too, in the early days of which I have to tell, he and a sister whose name——"

"Well?"

"Was Evelyn."

"Sweetwater, you are an admirable fellow. So the mystery is ours."

"The history, not the mystery; that still holds. Shall I relate what I know of those two families?"

"At once: I am as anxious as if I were again twenty-three and had been in your shoes instead of my own for the last three days."

"Very well, sir. John Poindexter and Amos Cadwalader were, in their early life, bosom friends. They had come from Scotland together and settled in Montgomery in the thirties. Both married there, but John Poindexter was a prosperous man from the first, while Cadwalader had little ability to support a family, and was on the verge of bankruptcy when the war of the rebellion broke out and he enlisted as a soldier. Poindexter remained at home, caring for his own family and for the two children of Cadwalader, whom he took into his own house. I say his own family, but he had no family, save a wife, up to the spring of '80. Then a daughter was born to him, the Eva who has just married Thomas Adams. Cadwalader, who was fitted for army life, rose to be a captain; but he was unfortunately taken prisoner at one of the late battles and confined in Libby Prison, where he suffered the tortures of the damned till he was released, in 1865, by a forced exchange of prisoners. Broken, old, and crushed, he returned home, and no one living in the town at that time will ever forget the day he alighted from the cars and took his way up the main street. For not having been fortunate enough, or unfortunate enough, perhaps, to receive any communication from home, he advanced with a cheerful haste, not knowing that his only daughter then lay dead in his friend's house, and that it was for her funeral that the people were collecting in the green square at the end of the street. He was so pale, broken, and decrepit that few knew him. But there was one old neighbor who recognized him and was kind enough to lead him into a quiet place, and there tell him that he had arrived just too late to see his darling daughter alive. The shock, instead of prostrating the old soldier, seemed to nerve him afresh and put new vigor into his limbs. He proceeded, almost on a run, to Poindexter's house, and arrived just as the funeral cortège was issuing from the door. And now happened a strange thing. The young girl had been laid on an open bier, and was being carried by six sturdy lads to her last resting place. As the father's eye fell on her young body under its black pall, a cry of mortal anguish escaped him, and he sank on his knees right in the line of the procession.

"At the same minute another cry went up, this time from behind the bier, and John Poindexter could be seen reeling at the side of Felix Cadwalader, who alone of all present (though he was the youngest and the least) seemed to retain his self-possession at this painful moment. Meanwhile the bereaved father, throwing himself at the side of the bier, began tearing away at the pall in his desire to look upon the face of her he had left in such rosy health four years before. But he was stopped, not by Poindexter, who had vanished from the scene, but by Felix, the cold, severe-looking boy who stood like a guard behind his sister. Reaching out a hand so white it was in itself a shock, he laid it in a certain prohibitory way on the pall, as if saying no. And when his father would have continued the struggle, it was Felix who controlled him and gradually drew him into the place at his own side where a minute before the imposing figure of Poindexter had stood; after which the bearers took up their burden again and moved on.

"But the dramatic scene was not over. As they neared the churchyard another procession, similar in appearance to their own, issued from an adjoining street, and Evelyn's young lover, who had died almost simultaneously with herself, was brought in and laid at her side. But not in the same grave: this was noticed by all, though most eyes and hearts were fixed upon Cadwalader, who had escaped his loathsome prison and returned to the place of his affections for *this*.

"Whether he grasped then and there the full meaning of this double burial (young Kissam had shot himself upon hearing of Evelyn's death), or whether all explanations were deferred till he and Felix walked away together from the grave, has never

- 76 -

transpired. From that minute till they both left town on the following day, no one had any word with him, save Poindexter, whom he went once to see, and young Kissam's mother, who came once to see him. Like a phantom he had risen upon the sight of the good people of Montgomery, and like a phantom he disappeared, never to be seen by any of them again, unless, as many doubt, the story is true which was told some twenty years ago by one of the little village lads. He says (it was six years after the tragic scene I have just related) that one evening as he was hurrying by the churchyard, in great anxiety to reach home before it was too dark, he came upon the figure of a man standing beside a grave, with a little child in his arms. This man was tall, long-bearded, and terrifying. His attitude, as the lad describes it, was one of defiance, if not of cursing. High in his right hand he held the child, almost as if he would hurl him at the village which lies under the hill on which the churchyard is perched; and though the moment passed quickly, the boy, now a man, never has forgotten the picture thus presented or admitted that it was anything but a real one. As the description he gave of this man answered to the appearance of Amos Cadwalader, and as the shoe of a little child was found next morning on the grave of Cadwalader's daughter, Evelyn, it has been thought by many that the boy really beheld this old soldier, who for some mysterious reason had chosen nightfall for this fleeting visit to his daughter's resting-place. But to others it was only a freak of the lad's imagination, which had been much influenced by the reading of romances. For, as these latter reasoned, had it really been Cadwalader, why did he not show himself at John Poindexter's house—that old friend who now had a little daughter and no wife and who could have made him so comfortable? Among these was Poindexter himself, though some thought he looked oddly while making this remark, as if he spoke more from custom than from the heart. Indeed, since the unfortunate death of Evelyn in his house, he had never shown the same interest in the Cadwaladers. But then he was a man much occupied with great affairs, while the Cadwaladers, except for their many griefs and misfortunes, were regarded as comparatively insignificant people, unless we except Felix, who from his earliest childhood had made himself feared even by grown people, though he never showed a harsh spirit or exceeded the bounds of decorum in speech or gesture. A year ago news came to Montgomery of

Amos Cadwalader's death, but no particulars concerning his family or burial place. And that is all I have been able to glean concerning the Cadwaladers."

Mr. Gryce had again become thoughtful.

"Have you any reason to believe that Evelyn's death was not a natural one?"

"No, sir. I interviewed the old mother of the young man who shot himself out of grief at Evelyn's approaching death, and if any doubt had existed concerning a matter which had driven her son to a violent end, she could not have concealed it from me. But there seemed to have been none. Evelyn Cadwalader was always of delicate health, and when a quick consumption carried her off no one marvelled. Her lover, who adored her, simply could not live without her, so he shot himself. There was no mystery about the tragic occurrence except that it seemed to sever an old friendship that once was firm as a rock. I allude to that between the Poindexters and Cadwaladers."

"Yet in this tragedy which has just occurred in —— Street we see them brought together again. Thomas Adams marries Eva Poindexter. But who is Thomas Adams? You have not mentioned him in this history."

"Not unless he was the child who was held aloft over Evelyn's grave."

"Humph! That seems rather far-fetched. What did you learn about him in Montgomery? Is he known there?"

"As well as any stranger can be who spends his time in courting a young girl. He came to Montgomery a few months ago, from some foreign city—Paris, I think—and, being gifted with every personal charm calculated to please a cultivated young woman, speedily won the affections of Eva Poindexter, and also the esteem of her father. But their favorable opinion is not shared by every one in the town. There are those who have a good deal to say about his anxious and unsettled eye."

"Naturally; he could not marry all their daughters. But this history you have given me: it is meagre, Sweetwater, and while it hints at something deeply tragic, does not supply the key we want. A girl who died some thirty years ago! A father who disappeared! A brother who, from being a Cadwalader, has become an Adams! An Eva whose name, as well as that of the long-buried Evelyn, was to be heard in constant repetition in the place where the murdered Felix lay with those inscrutable lines in his own writing, clinched between his teeth! It is a snarl, a perfect snarl, of which we have as yet failed to pull the right thread. But we'll get hold of it yet. I'm not going to be baffled in my old age by difficulties I would have laughed at a dozen years ago."

"But this right thread? How shall we know it among the fifty I see entangled in this matter?"

"First, find the whereabouts of this young couple—but didn't you tell me you had done so; that you know where they are?"

"Yes. I learned from the postmaster in Montgomery that a letter addressed to Mrs. Thomas Adams had been sent from his post-office to Belleville, Long Island."

"Ah! I know that place."

"And wishing to be assured that the letter was not a pretense, I sent a telegram to the postmaster at Belleville. Here is his answer. It is unequivocal: 'Mr. Poindexter of Montgomery, Pa. Mr. Thomas Adams and Mrs. Adams of the same place have been at the Bedell House in this place five days.'"

"Very good; then we have them! Be ready to start for Belleville by one o'clock sharp. And mind, Sweetwater, keep your wits alert and your tongue still. Remember that as yet we are feeling our way blindfold, and must continue to do so till some kind hand tears away the bandage from our eyes. Go! I have a letter to write, for which you may send in a boy at the end of five minutes."

This letter was for Miss Butterworth, and created, a half-hour later, quite a stir in the fine old mansion in Gramercy Park. It ran thus:

Have you sufficient interest in the outcome of a certain matter to take a short journey into the country? I leave town at 1 P.M. for Belleville, Long Island. If you choose to do the same, you will find me at the Bedell House, in that town, early in the afternoon. If you enjoy novels, take one with you, and let me see you reading it on the hotel piazza at five o'clock. I may be reading too; if so, and my choice is a book, all is well, and you may devour your story in peace. But if I lay aside my book and take up a paper, devote but one eye to your story and turn the other on the people who are passing you. If after you have done so, you leave your book open, I shall understand that you fail to recognize these persons. But if you shut the volume, you may expect to see me also fold up my newspaper; for by so doing you will have signaled me that you have identified the young man and woman you saw leaving Mr. Adams's house on the fatal afternoon of your first entrance. E. G.

CHAPTER XI

MISERY

It is to be hoped that the well-dressed lady of uncertain age who was to be seen late that afternoon in a remote corner of the hotel piazza at Belleville had not chosen a tale requiring great concentration of mind, for her eyes (rather fine ones in their way, showing both keenness and good nature) seemed to find more to interest them in the scene before her than in the pages she so industriously turned over.

The scene was one calculated to interest an idle mind, no doubt. First, there was the sea, a wide expanse of blue, dotted by numerous sails; then the beach, enlivened by groups of young people dressed like popinjays in every color; then the village street, and, lastly, a lawn over which there now and then strayed young couples with tennis rackets in their hands or golf sticks under their arms. Children, too—but children did not seem to interest this amiable spinster. (There could be no doubt about her being a spinster.) She scarcely glanced at them twice, while a young married pair, or even an old gentleman, if he were only tall and imperious-looking, invariably caused her eyes to wander from her book, which, by the way, she held too near for seeing, or such might have been the criticism of a wary observer.

This criticism, if criticism it would be called, could not have been made of the spruce, but rather feeble octogenarian at the other end of the piazza. He was evidently absorbed in the novel he held so conspicuously open, and which, from the smiles now and then disturbing the usual placidity of his benevolent features, we can take for granted was sufficiently amusing. Yet right in the midst of it, and certainly before he had finished his chapter, he closed his book and took out a newspaper, which he opened to its full width before sitting down to peruse its columns. At the same moment the lady at the other end of the piazza could be seen looking over her spectacles at two gentlemen who just at that moment issued from the great door opening between her and the elderly person just alluded to. Did she know them, or was it only her curiosity that was aroused? From the way she banged together her book and rose, it looked as if she had detected old acquaintances in the distinguished-looking pair who were now advancing slowly toward her. But if so, she could not have been overjoyed to see them, for after the first hint of their approach in her direction she turned, with an aspect of some embarrassment, and made her way out upon the lawn, where she stood with her back to these people, caressing a small dog in a way that betrayed her total lack of sympathy with these animals, which were evidently her terror when she was sufficiently herself to be swayed by her natural impulses.

The two gentlemen, on the contrary, with an air of total indifference to her proximity, continued their walk until they reached the end of the piazza, and then turned and proceeded mechanically to retrace their steps.

Their faces now being brought within view of the elderly person who was so absorbed in his newspaper, the latter shifted that sheet the merest trifle, possibly because the sun struck his eyes too directly, possibly because he wished to catch sight of two very remarkable men. If so, the opportunity was good, as they stopped within a few feet of his chair. One of them was elderly, as old as, if not older than, the man watching him; but he was of that famous Scotch stock whose members are tough and hale at eighty. This toughness he showed not only in his figure, which was both upright and graceful, but in the glance of his calm, cold eye, which fell upon everybody and everything unmoved, while that of his young, but equally stalwart companion seemed to shrink with the most acute sensitiveness from every person he met, save the very mild old reader of news near whom they now paused for a half-dozen words of conversation.

"I don't think it does me any good," was the young man's gloomy remark. "I am wretched when with her, and doubly wretched when I try to forget myself for a moment out of her sight. I think we had better go back. I had rather sit where she can see me than have her wonder—Oh, I will be careful; but you must remember how unnerving is the very silence I am obliged to keep about what is destroying us all. I am nearly as ill as she."

Here they drew off, and their apparently disinterested hearer turned the page of his paper. It was five minutes before they came back. This time it was the old gentleman who was speaking, and as he was more discreet than his companion or less under the influence of his feelings, his voice was lower and his words less easy to be distinguished.

"Escape? South coast—she will forget to watch you for—a clinging nature—impetuous, but foolishly affectionate—you know that—no danger—found out—time—a cheerful home—courage—happiness—all forgotten."

A gesture from the young man as he moved away showed that he did not share these hopes. Meanwhile Miss Butterworth—you surely have recognized Miss Butterworth—had her opportunities too. She was still stooping over the dog, which wriggled under her hand, yet did not offer to run away, fascinated perhaps by that hesitating touch which he may or may not have known had never inflicted itself upon a dog before. But her ears, and attention, were turned toward two girls chatting on a bench near her as freely as if they were quite alone on the lawn. They were gossiping about a fellow-inmate of the big hotel, and Miss Butterworth listened intently after hearing them mention the name Adams. These are some of the words she caught:

"But she is! I tell you she is sick enough to have a nurse and a doctor. I caught a glimpse of her as I was going by her room yesterday, and I never saw two such big eyes or such pale cheeks. Then, look at him! He must just adore her, for he won't speak to another woman, and just moves about in that small, hot room all day. I wonder if they are bride and groom? They are young enough, and if you have noticed her clothes——"

"Oh, don't talk about clothes. I saw her the first day she came, and was the victim of despair until she suddenly got sick and so couldn't wear those wonderful waists and jackets. I felt like a dowdy when I saw that pale blue——"

"Oh, well, blue becomes blondes. You would look like a fright in it. I didn't care about her clothes, but I did feel that it was all up with us if she chose to talk, or even to smile, upon the few men that are good enough to stay out a week in this place. Yet she isn't a beauty; she has not a good nose, nor a handsome eye, nor even an irreproachable complexion. It must be her mouth, which is lovely, or her walk—did you notice her walk? It was just as if she were floating; that is, before she fell down in that faint. I wonder why she fainted. Nobody was doing anything, not even her husband. But perhaps that was what troubled her. I noticed that for some cause he was looking very serious—and when she had tried to attract his attention two or three times and failed, she just fell from her chair to the floor. That roused him. He has hardly left her since."

"I don't think they look very happy, do you, for so rich and handsome a couple?"

"Perhaps he is dissipated. I have noticed that the old gentleman never leaves them."

"Well, well, he may be dissipated; handsome men are very apt to be. But I wouldn't care if——"

Here the dog gave a yelp and bolted. Miss Butterworth had unconsciously pinched him, in her indignation, possibly, at the turn these rattle-pated young ladies' conversation was taking. This made a diversion, and the young girls moved off, leaving Miss Butterworth without occupation. But a young man who at that moment crossed her path gave her enough to think about.

"You recognize them? There is no mistake?" he whispered.

"None; the one this way is the young man I saw leave Mr. Adams's house, and the other is the old gentleman who came in afterward."

"Mr. Gryce advises you to return home. He is going to arrest the young man." And Sweetwater passed on.

Miss Butterworth strolled to a seat and sat down. She felt weak; she seemed to see that young wife, sick, overwhelmed, struggling with her great fear, sink under this crushing blow, with no woman near her capable of affording the least sympathy. The father did not impress her as being the man to hold up her fainting head or ease her bruised heart. He had an icy look under his polished exterior which repelled this keen-eyed spinster, and as she remembered the coldness of his ways, she felt herself seized by an irresistible impulse to be near this young creature when the blow fell, if only to ease the tension of her own heartstrings, which at that moment ached keenly over the part she had felt herself obliged to play in this matter.

But when she rose to look for Mr. Gryce, she found him gone; and upon searching the piazza for the other two gentlemen, she saw them just vanishing round the corner in the direction of a small smoking-room. As she could not follow them, she went upstairs, and, meeting a maid in the upper hall, asked for Mrs. Adams. She was told that Mrs. Adams was sick, but was shown the door of her room, which was at the end of a long hall. As all the halls terminated in a window under which a sofa was to be found, she felt that circumstances were in her favor, and took her seat upon the sofa before her in a state of great complacency. Instantly a sweet voice was heard through the open transom of the door behind which her thoughts were already concentrated.

"Where is Tom? Oh, where is Tom? Why does he leave me? I'm afraid of what he may be tempted to do or say down on those great piazzas alone."

"Mr. Poindexter is with him," answered a voice, measured, but kind. "Mr. Adams was getting very tired, and your father persuaded him to go down and have a smoke."

"I must get up; indeed I must get up. Oh! the camphor—the——"

There was a bustle; this poor young wife had evidently fainted again.

Miss Butterworth cast very miserable glances at the door.

Meanwhile in that small and retired smoking-room a terrible scene was in progress. The two gentlemen had lit their cigars and were sitting in certain forced attitudes that evinced their non-enjoyment of the weed each had taken out of complaisance to the other, when an old man, strangely serious, strangely at home, yet as strangely a guest of the house like themselves, came in, and shut the door behind him.

"Gentlemen," he at once announced, "I am Detective Gryce of the New York police, and I am here—but I see that one of you at least knows why I am here."

One? Both of them! This was evident in a moment. No denial, no subterfuge was possible. At the first word uttered in the strange, authoritative tone which old detectives acquire after years of such experiences, the young man sank down in sudden collapse, while his companion, without yielding so entirely to his emotions, showed that he was not insensible to the blow which, in one moment, had brought destruction to all their hopes.

When Mr. Gryce saw himself so completely understood, he no longer hesitated over his duty. Directing his full attention to Mr. Adams, he said, this time with some feeling, for the misery of this young man had impressed him:

"You are wanted in New York by Coroner D——, whose business it is to hold an inquest over the remains of Mr. Felix Adams, of whose astonishing death you are undoubtedly informed. As you and your wife were seen leaving that gentleman's house a few minutes before he expired, you are naturally regarded as valuable witnesses in determining whether his death was one of suicide or murder."

It was an accusation, or so nearly one, that Mr. Gryce was not at all surprised to behold the dark flush of shame displace the livid terror which but an instant before had made the man before him look like one of those lost spirits we sometimes imagine as flitting across the open mouth of hell. But he said nothing, seemingly had no power to do so, and his father-in-law was about to make some effort to turn aside this blow when a voice in the hall outside was heard inquiring for Mr. Adams, saying that his wife had fainted again and required his help.

The young husband started, cast a look full of despair at Mr. Poindexter, and thrusting his hand against the door as if to hold it shut, sank on his knees before Mr. Gryce, saying:

"She knows! She suspects! Her nature is so sensitive."

This he managed to utter in gasps as the detective bent compassionately over him. "Don't, don't disturb her! She is an angel, a saint from heaven. Let me bear the blame—he was my brother—let me go with you, but leave her in ignorance——"

Mr. Gryce, with a vivid sense of justice, laid his hand on the young man's arm.

"Say nothing," he enjoined. "My memory is good, and I would rather hear nothing from your lips. As for your wife, my warrant does in no way include her; and if you promise to come with me quietly, I will even let you bid her adieu, so that you do it in my presence."

The change which passed over the young man's face at these significant words was of a nature to surprise Mr. Gryce. Rising slowly, he took his stand by Mr. Poindexter, who, true to his inflexible nature, had scarcely moved in limb and feature since Mr. Gryce came in.

"What have you against me?" he demanded. And there was a surprising ring to his voice, as if courage had come with the necessity of the moment. "Of what am I accused? I want you to tell me. I had rather you would tell me in so many words. I cannot leave in peace until you do."

Mr. Poindexter made a movement at this, and cast a half-suspicious, half-warning glance at his son-in-law. But the young man took no notice of his interference. He kept his eye on the detective, who quietly took out his warrant.

At this instant the door shook.

"Lock it!" was the hoarse command of the accused man. "Don't let any one pass that door, even if it is to bring the tidings of my wife's death."

Mr. Gryce reached out his hand, and turned the key in the lock. Young Adams opened the paper which he had taken from the detective's hand, and while his blood-shot eyes vainly sought to master the few lines there written, Mr. Poindexter attracted the attention of Mr. Gryce, and, fixing him with his eye, formed his lips with three soundless words:

"For murder? Him?"

The detective's bow and a very long-drawn sigh from his son-in-law answered him simultaneously. With a curious lift of his upper lip, which showed his teeth somewhat unpleasantly for a moment, he drew back a step, and sank into his previous immobility.

"I am indebted to you," declared the young man. "Now I know where I stand. I am quite ready to go with you and stand trial, if such be deemed necessary by the officials in New York. You," he cried, turning with almost an air of command to the old gentleman beside him, "will watch over Eva. Not like a father, sir, but like a mother. You will be at her side when she wakes, and, if possible, leave her only when she sleeps. Do not let her suffer—not too much. No newspapers, no gossiping women. Watch! watch! as I would watch, and when I come back—for I will come back, will I not?" he appealed to Mr. Gryce, "my prayers will bless you and——" A sob stuck in his throat, and he turned for a minute aside; then he took the detective's arm quite calmly and remarked:

"I do not want to say good-by to my wife. I cannot bear it. I had rather go straight from here without another glance at her unconscious face. When I have told my story, for I shall tell it to the first man who asks me, I may find courage to write her. Meanwhile, get me away as quickly as you can. Time enough for the world to know my shame to-morrow."

Mr. Gryce tapped on the window overlooking the piazza. A young man stepped in.

"Here is a gentleman," he cried, "who finds himself forced to return in great haste to New York. See that he gets to the train in time, without fuss and without raising the least comment. I will follow with his portmanteau. Mr. Poindexter, you are now at liberty to attend your suffering daughter." And with a turn of the key, he unlocked the door, and one of the most painful scenes of his long life was over.

CHAPTER XII

THOMAS EXPLAINS

Mr. Gryce was not above employing a little finesse. He had expressed his intention of following Mr. Adams, and he did follow him, but so immediately that he not only took the same train, but sat in the same car. He wished to note at his leisure the bearing of this young man, who interested him in quite a different way from what he had anticipated, a way that vaguely touched his own conscience and made him feel his years as he had no right to feel them when he had just brought to an end an intricate and difficult pursuit.

Seated at a distance, he watched with increasing interest the changes which passed over his prisoner's handsome countenance. He noted the calmness which now marked the features he had so lately seen writhing in deepest agony, and wondered from what source the strength came which enabled this young man to sit so stoically under the eyes of people from whose regard, an hour before, he had shrunk with such apparent suffering. Was it that courage comes with despair? Or was he too absorbed in his own misery to note the shadow it cast about him? His brooding brow and vacant eye spoke of a mind withdrawn from present surroundings. Into what depths of remorse, who could say? Certainly not this old detective, seasoned though he was by lifelong contact with criminals, some of them of the same social standing and cultured aspect as this young man.

At the station in Brooklyn he rejoined his prisoner, who scarcely looked up as he approached. In another hour they were at Police Headquarters and the serious questioning of Mr. Adams had begun.

He did not attempt to shirk it. Indeed, he seemed anxious to talk. He had a burden on his mind, and longed to throw it off. But the burden was not of the exact nature anticipated by the police. He did not acknowledge having killed his brother, but confessed to having been the incidental cause of that brother's death. The story he told was this:

"My name is Cadwalader, not Adams. My father, a Scotchman by birth, was a naturalized citizen of Pennsylvania, having settled in a place called Montgomery when a young married man. He had two children then, one of whom died in early life; the other was my brother Felix, whose violent death under the name of Adams you have called me here to explain. I am the fruit of a later marriage, entered into by my father some years after leaving Montgomery. When I was born he was living in Harrisburg, but, as he left there shortly after I had reached my third year, I have no remembrances connected with that city. Indeed, my recollections are all of very different scenes than this country affords. My mother having died while I was still an infant, I was sent very early in life to the Old World, from which my father had originally come. When I returned, which was not till this very year, I found my father dying, and my brother a grown man with money—a great deal of money—which I had been led to think he was ready to share with me. But after my father was laid away, Felix" (with what effort he uttered that name!) "Felix came to New York, and I was left to wander about without settled hopes or any definite promise of means upon which to base a future or start a career. While wandering, I came upon the town where my father had lived in early youth, and, hunting up his old friends, I met in the house of one who had come over from Scotland with my father a young lady" (how his voice shook, and with what a poignant accent he uttered that beloved name) "in whom I speedily became interested to the point of wishing to marry her. But I had no money, no business, no home to give her, and, as I was fain to acknowledge, no prospects. Still I could not give up the hope of making her my wife. So I wrote to my brother, Felix Cadwalader, or, rather, Felix Adams, as he preferred to be called in later years for family reasons entirely disconnected with the matter of his sudden demise, and, telling him I had become interested in a young girl of good family and some wealth, asked him to settle upon me a certain sum which would enable me to marry her with some feeling of self-respect. My only answer was a repetition of the vague promise he had thrown out before. But youth is hopeful, even to daring, and I decided to make her mine without further parley, in the hope that her beauty and endearing qualities would win from him, at first view, the definite concession he had so persistently denied me.

"This I did, and the fault with which I have most to reproach myself is that I entered into this alliance without taking her or her father into my confidence. They thought me well off, possibly rich, and while Mr. Poindexter is a man of means, I am sure, if he had known I had nothing but the clothes I wore and the merest trifle in the way of pocket money, he would have cried halt to the marriage, for he is a very ambitious man and considers his daughter well worth a millionaire's devotion—as she is.

"Felix (you must pardon me if I show no affection for my brother—he was a very strange man) was notified of my marriage, but did not choose to witness it, neither did he choose to prohibit it; so it was conducted quietly, with strangers for witnesses, in a hotel parlor. Then, with vague hopes, as well as certain vague fears, I prepared to take my young bride into the presence of my brother, who, hardened as he was by years of bachelorhood, could not be so entirely impervious to feminine charms as not to recognize my wife as a woman deserving of every consideration.

"But I had counted without my host. When, two days after the ceremony which had made us one, I took her to the house which has since become so unhappily notorious, I found that my brother had but shown me one facet, and that the least obdurate, of his many-sided nature.

"Brilliant as steel, he was as hard, and not only professed himself unmoved by my wife's many charms, but also as totally out of sympathy with such follies as love and marriage, which were, he said, the fruit of unoccupied minds and a pastime wholly unworthy of men boasting of such talents and attainments as ourselves. Then he turned his back upon us, and I, moved by an anger little short of frenzy, began an abuse for which he was so little prepared that he crouched like a man under blows, and, losing minute by minute his self-control, finally caught up a dagger lying close at hand, and crying, 'You want my money? Well, then, take it!' stabbed himself to the heart with one desperate blow.

"I fear I shall not be believed, but that is the story of this crime, gentlemen."

CHAPTER XIII

DESPAIR

Was it? Tragedies as unpremeditated as this had doubtless occurred, and inconsistencies in character shown themselves in similar impetuosities, from the beginning of time up till now. Yet there was not a man present, with or without the memory of Bartow's pantomime, which, as you will recall, did not tally at all with this account of Mr. Adams's violent end, who did not show in a greater or less degree his distrust and evident disbelief in this tale, poured out with such volubility before them.

The young man, gifted as he was with the keenest susceptibilities, perceived this, and his head drooped.

"I shall add nothing to and take nothing from what I have said," was his dogged remark. "Make of it what you will."

The inspector who was conducting the inquiry glanced dubiously at Mr. Gryce as these words left Thomas Adams's lips; whereupon the detective said:

"We are sorry you have taken such a resolution. There are many things yet left to be explained, Mr. Adams; for instance, why, if your brother slew himself in this unforeseen manner, you left the house so precipitately, without giving an alarm or even proclaiming your relationship to him?"

"You need not answer, you know," the inspector's voice broke in. "No man is called upon to incriminate himself in this free and independent country."

A smile, the saddest ever seen, wandered for a minute over the prisoner's pallid lips. Then he lifted his head and replied with a certain air of desperation:

"Incrimination is not what I fear now. From the way you all look at me I perceive that I am lost, for I have no means of proving my story."

This acknowledgment, which might pass for the despairing cry of an innocent man, made his interrogator stare.

"You forget," suggested that gentleman, "that you had your wife with you. She can corroborate your words, and will prove herself, no doubt, an invaluable witness in your favor."

"My wife!" he repeated, choking so that his words could be barely understood. "Must she be dragged into this—so sick, so weak a woman? It would kill her, sir. She loves me—she——"

"Was she with you in Mr. Adams's study? Did she see him lift the dagger against his own breast?"

"No." And with this denial the young man seemed to take new courage. "She had fainted several moments previously, while the altercation between my brother and myself was at its height. She did not see the final act, and—gentlemen, I might as well speak the truth (I have nothing to gain by silence), she finds it as difficult as you do to believe that Mr. Adams struck himself. I—I have tried with all my arts to impress the truth upon her, but oh, what can I hope from the world when the wife of my bosom—an angel, too, who loves me—oh, sirs, she can never be a witness for me; she is too conscientious, too true to her own convictions. I should lose—she would die——"

Mr. Gryce tried to stop him; he would not be stopped.

"Spare me, sirs! Spare my wife! Write me down guilty, anything you please, rather than force that young creature to speak——"

Here the inspector cut short these appeals which were rending every heart present. "Have you read the newspapers for the last few days?" he asked.

"I? Yes, yes, sir. How could I help it? Blood is blood; the man was my brother; I had left him dying—I was naturally anxious, naturally saw my own danger, and I read them, of course."

"Then you know he was found with a large cross on his breast, a cross which was once on the wall. How came it to be torn down? Who put it on his bosom?"

"I, sir. I am not a Catholic but Felix was, and seeing him dying without absolution, without extreme unction, I thought of the holy cross, and tore down the only one I saw, and placed it in his arms."

"A pious act. Did he recognize it?"

"I cannot say. I had my fainting wife to look after. She occupied all my thoughts."

"I see, and you carried her out and were so absorbed in caring for her you did not observe Mr. Adams's valet——"

"He's innocent, sir. Whatever people may think, he had nothing to do with this crime——"

"You did not observe him, I say, standing in the doorway and watching you?"

Now the inspector knew that Bartow had not been standing there, but at the loophole above; but the opportunity for entrapping the witness was too good to lose.

Mr. Adams was caught in the trap, or so one might judge from the beads of perspiration which at that moment showed themselves on his pale forehead. But he struggled to maintain the stand he had taken, crying hotly:

"But that man is crazy, and deaf-and-dumb besides! or so the papers give out. Surely his testimony is valueless. You would not confront me with him?"

"We confront you with no one. We only asked you a question. You did not observe the valet, then?"

"No, sir."

"Or understand the mystery of the colored lights?"

"No, sir."

"Or of the plate of steel and the other contrivances with which your brother enlivened his solitude?"

"I do not follow you, sir." But there was a change in his tone.

"I see," said the inspector, "that the complications which have disturbed us and made necessary this long delay in the collection of testimony have not entered into the crime as described by you. Now this is possible; but there is still a circumstance requiring explanation; a little circumstance, which is, nevertheless, one of importance, since your wife mentioned it to you as soon as she became conscious. I allude to the half dozen or more words which were written by your brother immediately preceding his death. The paper on which they were written has been found, and that it was a factor in your quarrel is evident, since she regretted that it had been left behind you, and he—Do you know where we found this paper?"

The eyes which young Adams raised at this interrogatory had no intelligence in them. The sight of this morsel of paper seemed to have deprived him in an instant of all the faculties with which he had been carrying on this unequal struggle. He shook his head, tried to reach out his hand, but failed to grasp the scrap of paper which the inspector held out. Then he burst into a loud cry:

"Enough! I cannot hold out, with no other support than a wicked lie. I killed my brother for reasons good as any man ever had for killing another. But I shall not impart them. I would rather be tried for murder and hanged."

It was a complete breakdown, pitiful from its contrast with the man's herculean physique and fine, if contracted, features. If the end, it was a sad end, and Mr. Gryce, whose forehead had taken on a deep line between the eyebrows, slowly rose and took his stand by the young man, who looked ready to fall. The inspector, on the contrary, did not move. He had begun a tattoo with his fingers on the table, and seemed bound to beat it out, when another sudden cry broke from the young man's lips:

"What is that?" he demanded, with his eyes fixed on the door, and his whole frame shaking violently.

"Nothing," began the inspector, when the door suddenly opened and the figure of a woman white as a wraith and wonderful with a sort of holy passion darted from the grasp of a man who sought to detain her, and stood before them, palpitating with a protest which for a moment she seemed powerless to utter.

It was Adams's young, invalid wife, whom he had left three hours before at Belleville. She was so frail of form, so exquisite of feature, that she would have seemed some unearthly visitant but for the human anguish which pervaded her look and soon found vent in this touching cry:

"What is he saying? Oh, I know well what he is saying. He is saying that he killed his brother, that he held the dagger which rid the world of a monster of whose wickedness none knew. But you must not heed him. Indeed you must not heed him. He is innocent; I, his wife, have come twenty miles, from a bed of weakness and suffering, to tell you so. He——"

But here a hand was laid gently, but firmly on her mouth. She looked up, met her husband's eyes filled with almost frantic appeal, and giving him a look in return that sank into the heart of every man who beheld it, laid her own hand on his and drew it softly away.

"It is too late, Tom, I must speak. My father, my own weakness, or your own peremptory commands could not keep me at Belleville when I knew you had been brought here. And shall I stop now, in the presence of these men who have heard your words and may believe them? No, that would be a cowardice unworthy of our love and the true lives we hope to lead together. Sirs!" and each man there held his breath to catch the words which came in faint and fainter intonation from her lips, "I know my husband to be innocent, because the hand that held the dagger was mine. I killed Felix Cadwalader!"

The horror of such a moment is never fully realized till afterward. Not a man there moved, not even her husband, yet on every cheek a slow pallor was forming, which testified to the effect of such words from lips made for smiles and showing in every curve the habit of gentle thought and the loftiest instincts. Not till some one cried out from the doorway, "Catch her! she is falling!" did any one stir or release the pent-up breath which awe and astonishment had hitherto held back on every lip. Then he in whose evident despair all could read the real cause of the great dread which had drawn him into a false confession, sprang forward, and with renewed life showing itself in every feature, caught her in his arms. As he staggered with her to a sofa and laid her softly down, he seemed another man in look and bearing; and Mr. Gryce, who had been watching the whole wonderful event with the strongest interest, understood at once the meaning of the change which had come over his prisoner at that point in his memorable arrest when he first realized that it was for himself they had come, and not for the really guilty person, the idolized object of his affections.

Meanwhile, he was facing them all, with one hand laid tenderly on that unconscious head.

"Do not think," he cried, "that because this young girl has steeped her hand in blood, she is a wicked woman. There is no purer heart on earth than hers, and none more worthy of the worship of a true man. See! she killed my brother, son of my father, beloved by my mother, yet I can kiss her hand, kiss her forehead, her eyes, her feet, not because I hate him, but because I worship her, the purest—the best——" He left her, and came and stood before those astonished men. "Sirs!" he cried, "I must ask you to listen to a strange, a terrible tale."

CHAPTER XIV

MEMORANDA

"It is like and unlike what I have just related to you," began young Adams. "In my previous confession I mixed truth and falsehood, and to explain myself fully and to help you to a right understanding of my wife's act, I shall have to start afresh and speak as if I had already told you nothing."

"Wait!" cried Mr. Gryce, in an authoritative manner. "We will listen to you presently;" and, leaning over the inspector, he whispered a few words, after which he took out a pencil and jotted down certain sentences, which he handed over to this gentleman.

As they had the appearance of a memorandum, and as the inspector glanced more than once at them while Mr. Adams (or Cadwalader, as he should now rightfully be called) was proceeding with his story, I will present them to you as written.

Points to be made clear by Mr. Adams in his account of this crime:

1. Why a woman who was calm enough to stop and arrange her hair during the beginning of an interview should be wrought up to such a pitch of frenzy and exasperation before it was over as to kill with her own hand a man against whom she had evidently no previous grudge. (Remember the comb found on the floor of Mr. Adams's bedroom.)

2. What was the meaning of the following words, written just previous to this interview by the man thus killed: "I return you your daughter. Neither you nor she shall ever see me again. Remember Evelyn!"

3. Why was the pronoun "I" used in this communication? What position did Mr. Felix Adams hold toward this young girl qualifying him to make use of such language after her marriage to his brother?

4. And having used it, why did he, upon being attacked by her, attempt to swallow the paper upon which he had written these words, actually dying with it clinched between his teeth?

5. If he was killed in anger and died as monsters do (her own word), why did his face show sorrow rather than hate, and a determination as far as possible removed from the rush of over-whelming emotions likely to follow the reception of a mortal blow from the hand of an unexpected antagonist?

6. Why, if he had strength to seize the above-mentioned paper and convey it to his lips, did he not use that strength in turning on a light calculated to bring him assistance, instead of leaving blazing the crimson glow which, according to the code of signals as now understood by us, means: "Nothing more required just now. Keep away."

7. What was the meaning of the huge steel plate found between the casings of the doorway, and why did it remain at rest within its socket at this, the culminating moment of his life?

8. An explanation of how old Poindexter came to appear on the scene so soon after the event. His words as overheard were: "It is Amos's son, not Amos!" Did he not know whom he was to meet in this house? Was the condition of the man lying before him with a cross on his bosom and a dagger in his heart less of a surprise to him than the personality of the victim?

9. Remember the conclusions we have drawn from Bartow's pantomime. Mr. Adams was killed by a left-handed thrust. Watch for an acknowledgment that the young woman is left-handed, and do not forget that an explanation is due why for so long a time she held her other arm stretched out behind her.

10. Why did the bird whose chief cry is "Remember Evelyn!" sometimes vary it with "Poor Eva! Lovely Eva! Who would strike Eva?" The story of this tragedy, to be true, must show that Mr. Adams knew his brother's bride both long and well.

11. If Bartow is, as we think, innocent of all connection with this crime save as witness, why does he show such joy at its result? This may not reasonably be expected to fall within the scope of Thomas Adams's confession, but it should not be ignored by us. This deaf-

and-dumb servitor was driven mad by a fact which caused him joy. Why?

12. Notice the following schedule. It has been drawn up after repeated experiments with Bartow and the various slides of the strange lamp which cause so many different lights to shine out in Mr. Adams's study:

White light—Water wanted.Green light—Overcoat and hat to be brought.Blue light—Put back books on shelves.Violet light— Arrange study for the night.Yellow light—Watch for next light.Red light—Nothing wanted; stay away.

The last was on at the final scene. Note if this fact can be explained by Mr. Adams's account of the same.

With these points in our mind, let us peruse the history of this crime and of the remote and possibly complicated causes which led to it.

BOOK II

REMEMBER EVELYN

CHAPTER I

THE SECRET OF THE CADWALADERS

Thomas Cadwalader suggested rather than told his story. We dare not imitate him in this, nor would it be just to your interest to relate these facts with all the baldness and lack of detail imposed upon this unhappy man by the hurry and anxiety of the occasion. Remarkable tragedies have their birth in remarkable facts, and as such facts are but the outcome of human passions, we must enter into those passions if we would understand either the facts or their appalling consequences. In this case, the first link of the chain which led to Felix Adams's violent death was forged before the birth of the woman who struck him. We must begin, then, with almost forgotten days, and tell the story, as her pleader did, from the standpoint of Felix and Thomas Cadwalader.

Thomas Cadwalader—now called Adams—never knew his mother; she died in his early infancy. Nor could he be said to have known his father, having been brought up in France by an old Scotch lawyer, who, being related to his mother, sometimes spoke of her, but never of his father, till Thomas had reached his fifteenth year. Then he put certain books into his hands, with this remarkable injunction:

"Here are romances, Thomas. Read them; but remember that none of them, no matter how thrilling in matter or effect, will ever equal the story of your father's bitterly wronged and suffering life."

"My father!" he cried; "tell me about him; I have never heard."

But his guardian, satisfied with an allusion which he knew must bear fruit in the extremely susceptible nature of this isolated boy, said no more that day, and Thomas turned to the books. But nothing after that could ever take his mind away from his father. He had scarcely thought of him for years, but now that that father had been placed before him in the light of a wronged man, he found himself continually hunting back in the deepest recesses of his memory for some long-forgotten recollection of that father's features calculated to restore his image to his eyes. Sometimes he succeeded in this, or thought he did; but this image, if image it was, was so speedily lost in a sensation of something strange and awe-compelling enveloping it, that he found himself more absorbed by the intangible impressions associated with this memory than by the memory itself. What were these impressions, and in what had they originated? In vain he tried to determine. They were as vague as they were persistent. A stretch of darkness—two bars of orange light, always shining, always the same—black lines against these bars, like the tops of distant gables—an inner thrill—a vague affright—a rush about him as of a swooping wind—all this came with his father's image, only to fade away with it, leaving him troubled, uneasy, and perplexed. Finding these impressions persistent, and receiving no explanation of them in his own mind, he finally asked his guardian what they meant. But that guardian was as ignorant as himself on this topic; and satisfied with having roused the boy's imagination, confined himself to hints, dropped now and then with a judiciousness which proved the existence of a deliberate purpose, of some duty which awaited him on the other side of the water, a duty which would explain his long exile from his only parent and for which he must fit himself by study and the acquirement of such accomplishments as render a young man a positive power in society, whether that society be of the Old World or the New. He showed his shrewdness in thus dealing with this pliable and deeply affectionate nature. From this time forth Thomas felt himself leading a life of mystery and interest.

To feel himself appointed for a work whose unknown character only heightened its importance gave point to every effort now made by this young man, and lent to his studies that vague touch of romance which made them a delight, and him an adept in many things he might otherwise have cared little about. At eighteen he was a graduate from the Sorbonne, and a musical virtuoso as well. He could fence, ride, and carry off the prize in games requiring physical prowess as well as mental fitness. He was, in fact, a prodigy in many ways, and was so considered by his fellow-students. He, however, was not perfect; he lacked social charm, and in so far failed of being the complete gentleman. This he was made to realize in the following way:

One morning his guardian came to him with a letter from his father, in which, together with some words of commendation for his present attainments, that father expressed a certain dissatisfaction with his general manner as being too abrupt and self-satisfied with those of his own sex, and much too timid and deprecatory with those of the other. Thomas felt the criticism and recognized its justice; but how had his father, proved by his letter to be no longer a myth, become acquainted with defects which Thomas instinctively felt could never have attracted the attention of his far from polished guardian?

His questions on this point elicited a response that confounded him. He was not the only son of his father; he had a brother living, and this brother, older than himself by some twenty years or more, had just been in Paris, where, in all probability, he had met him, talked with him, and perhaps pressed his hand.

It was a discovery calculated to deepen the impression already made upon Thomas's mind. Only a purpose of the greatest importance could account for so much mystery. What could it be? What was he destined to do or say or be? He was not told, but while awaiting enlightenment he was resolved not to be a disappointment to the two anxious souls who watched his career so eagerly and exacted from him such perfection. He consequently moderated his manner, and during the following year acquired by constant association with the gilded youth about him that indescribable charm of the perfect gentleman which he was led to believe would alone meet with the approval of those he now felt bound to please. At the end of the year he found himself a finished man of the world. How truly so, he began to realize when he noted the blush with which his presence was hailed by women and the respect shown him by men of his own stamp. In the midst of the satisfaction thus experienced his guardian paid him a final visit.

"You are now ready," said he, "for your father's summons. It will come in a few weeks. Be careful, then. Form no ties you cannot readily break; for, once recalled from France, you are not likely to return here. What your father's purpose concerning you may be I do not know, but it is no ordinary one. You will have money, a well-appointed home, family affection, all that you have hitherto craved in vain, and in return you will carry solace to a heart which has awaited your healing touch for twenty years. So much I am ordered to say; the rest you will hear from your father's own lips."

Aroused, encouraged, animated by the wildest hopes, the most extravagant anticipations, Thomas awaited his father's call with feverish impatience, and when it came, hastened to respond to it by an immediate voyage to America. This was some six months previous to the tragedy in ---- Street. On his arrival at the wharf in New York he was met, not by his brother, as he had every reason to expect, but by a messenger in whose face evil tidings were apparent before he spoke. Thomas was soon made acquainted with them. His father, who he now learned was called Cadwalader (he himself had always been called Adams), was ill, possibly dying. He must therefore hasten, and, being provided with minute instructions as to his way, took the train at once for a small village in northern Pennsylvania.

All that followed was a dream to him. He was hurried through the night, with the motion of the ship still in his blood, to meet— what? He dared not think. He swam in a veritable nightmare. Then came a stop, a hurrying from the train, a halt on a platform reeking with rain (for the night was stormy), a call from some one to hurry, the sight of a panting horse steaming under a lamp whose blowing flame he often woke in after nights to see, a push from a persuasive hand, then a ride over a country road the darkness of which seemed impenetrable, and, finally, the startling vision of an open door, with a Meg Merrilies of a woman standing in it, holding a flaming candle in her hand. The candle went out while he looked at it, and left only a voice to guide him—a voice which, in tones shaken by chill or feeling, he could not tell which, cried eagerly:

"Is that you, laddie? Come awa in. Come awa in. Dinna heed the rain. The maister's been crying on you a' day. I'm glad you're no ower late."

He got down, followed the voice, and, stumbling up a step or two, entered a narrow door, which was with difficulty held open behind him, and which swung to with a loud noise the minute he crossed the threshold. This or the dreariness of the place in which he found himself disturbed him greatly. Bare floors, stained walls, meagre doorways, and a common pine staircase, lighted only by the miserable candle which the old woman had relit—were these the appointments of the palatial home he had been led to expect? These the surroundings, this the abode of him who had exacted such perfection on his part, and to satisfy whose standard he had devoted years of hourly, daily effort, in every department of art and science? A sickening revolt seized him, aggravated by the smiles of the old woman, who dipped and courtesied before him in senile delight. She may have divined his feelings, for, drawing him inside, she relieved him of his overcoat, crying all the while, with an extravagant welcome more repulsive than all the rest:

"O the fine laddie! Wad your puir mither could see you the noo! Bonnie and clever! No your faither's bairn ava! All mither, laddie, all mither!"

The room was no better than the hall.

"Where is my father?" he asked, authoritatively, striving to keep down his strong repugnance.

"Dinna ye hear him? He's crying on ye. Puir man, he's wearying to see ye."

Hear him? He could scarcely hear her. The driving rain, the swish of some great boughs against the house, the rattling of casements and doors, and the shrieking of wind in the chimney made all other sounds wellnigh inaudible. Yet as he listened he seemed to catch the accents of a far-off voice calling, now wistfully, now imperatively, "Thomas! Thomas!" And, thrilled with an emotion almost superstitious in its intensity, he moved hastily toward the staircase.

But the old woman was there before him. "Na! Na!" she cried. "Come in by and eat something first."

But Thomas shook his head. It seemed to him at that moment as if he never could eat or sleep again, the disillusion was so bitter, his disappointment so keen.

"You will na? Then haste ye—haste ye. But it's a peety you wadna ha'e eaten something. Ye'll need it, laddie; ye'll need it."

"Thomas! Thomas!" wailed the voice.

He tore himself away. He forced himself to go upstairs, following the cry, which at every moment grew louder. At the top he cast a final glance below. The old woman stood at the stair-foot, shading the candle from the draught with a hand that shook with something more than age. She was gazing after him in vague affright, and with the shadow of this fear darkening her weazen face, formed a picture from which he was glad to escape.

Plunging on, he found himself before a window whose small panes dripped and groaned under a rain that was fast becoming a torrent. Chilled by the sight, he turned toward the door faintly outlined beside it, and in the semi-darkness seized an old-fashioned latch rattling in the wind that permeated every passageway, and softly raised it.

Instantly the door fell back, and two eyes blazing with fever and that fire of the soul of which fever is the mere physical symbol greeted him from the midst of a huge bed drawn up against the opposite wall. Then two arms rose, and the moaning cry of "Thomas! Thomas!" changed to a shout, and he knew himself to be in the presence of his father.

Falling on his knees in speechless emotion, he grasped the wasted hands held out to him. Such a face, rugged though it was and far from fulfilling the promise held out to him in his dreams, could not but move any man. As he gazed into it and pressed the hands in which the life blood only seemed to linger for this last, this only embrace, all his filial instincts were aroused and he forgot the common surroundings, the depressing rain, his own fatigue and bitter disappointment, in his lifelong craving for love and family recognition.

But the old man on whose breast he fell showed other emotions than those by which he was himself actuated. It was not an embrace he craved, but an opportunity to satisfy an almost frenzied curiosity as to the appearance and attributes of the son who had grown to manhood under other eyes. Pushing him gently back, he bade him stand in the light of the lamp burning on a small pine table, and surveyed him, as it were, from the verge of his own fast failing life, with moans of mingled pain and weariness, amid which Thomas thought he heard the accents of a supreme satisfaction.

Meanwhile in Thomas himself, as he stood there, the sense of complete desolation filled his breast almost to bursting. To have come home for this! To find a father only to be weighed in the scales of that father's judgment! To be admired, instead of loved!

As he realized his position and listened to the shrieking of the wind and rain, he felt that the wail of the elements but echoed the cry of his own affections, thus strangled in their birth. Indeed the sensations of that moment made so deep an impression upon him that he was never afterward able to hear a furious gust of wind or rain without the picture rising up before him of this great hollow room, with the trembling figure of his father struggling in the grasp of death and holding it at bay, while he gauged with worldly wisdom the physical, mental, and moral advantages of the son so long banished and so lately restored to his arms.

A rush of impetuous words followed by the collapse of his father's form upon the pillow showed that the examination was over. Rushing forward, he grasped again that father's hands, but soon shrank back, stunned by what he heard and the prospect it opened before him. A few of his father's words will interpret the rest. They came in a flood, and among others Thomas caught these:

"The grace of God be thanked! Our efforts have not failed. Handsome, strong, noble in look and character, we could ask nothing more, hope for nothing more. My revenge will succeed! John Poindexter will find that he has a heart, and that that heart can be wrung. I do not need to live to see it. For me it exists now; it exists here!" And he struck his breast with hands that seemed to have reserved their last strength for this supreme gesture.

John Poindexter! Who was he? It was a new name to Thomas. Venturing to say so, he reeled under the look he received from his father's eyes.

"You do not know who John Poindexter is, and what he has done to me and mine? They have kept their promise well, too well, but God will accord me strength to tell you what has been left unsaid by them. He would not bring me up to this hour to let me perish before you have heard the story destined to make you the avenger of innocence upon that enemy of your race. Listen, Thomas. With the hand of death encircling my heart, I speak, and if the story find you cold—But it will not. Your name is Cadwalader, and it will not."

Constrained by passions such as he had never imagined even in dreams, Thomas fell upon his knees. He could not listen otherwise. His father, gasping for breath, fixed him with his hollow eyes, in which the last flickering flames of life flared up in fitful brightness.

"Thomas"—the pause was brief—"you are not my only child."

"I know it," fell from Thomas's white lips. "I have a brother; his name is Felix."

The father shook his head with a look suggestive of impatience.

"Not him! Not him!" he cried. "A sister! a sister, who died before you were born—beautiful, good, with a voice like an angel's and a heart—she should be standing by my side to-day, and she would have been if—if he—but none of that. I have no breath to waste. Facts, facts, just facts! Afterward may come emotions, hatred, denunciation, not now. This is my story, Thomas.

"John Poindexter and I were friends. From boyhood we shared each other's bed, food, and pleasures, and when he came to seek his fortune in America I accompanied him. He was an able man, but cold. I was of an affectionate nature, but without any business capacity. As proof of this, in fifteen years he was rich, esteemed, the master of a fine house, and the owner of half a dozen horses; while I was the same nobody I had been at first, or would have been had not Providence given me two beautiful children and blessed, or rather cursed, me with the friendship of this prosperous man. When Felix was fourteen and Evelyn three years older, their mother died. Soon after, the little money I had vanished in an unfortunate enterprise, and life began to promise ill, both for myself and for my growing children. John Poindexter, who was honest enough then, or let me hope so, and who had no children of his own, though he had been long married, offered to take one of mine to educate. But I did not consent to this till the war of the rebellion broke out; then I sent him both son and daughter, and went into the army. For four years I fought for the flag, suffering all that a man can suffer and live, and being at last released from Libby Prison, came home with a heart full of gratitude and with every affection keyed up by a long series of unspeakable experiences, to greet my son and clasp once more within my wasted arms the idolized form of my deeply loved daughter. What did I find? A funeral in the streets—hers—and Felix, your brother, walking like a guard between her speechless corpse and the man under whose protection I had placed her youth and innocence.

"Betrayed!" shrieked the now frenzied parent, rising on his pillow. "Her innocence! Her sweetness! And he, cold as the stone we laid upon her grave, had seen her perish with the anguish and shame of it, without a sign of grief or a word of contrition."

"O God!" burst from lips the old man was watching with frenzied cunning.

"Ay, God!" repeated the father, shaking his head as if in defiance before he fell back on his pillow. "He allowed it and I—But this does not tell the story. I must keep to facts as Felix did—Felix, who was but fifteen years old and yet found himself the only confidant and solace of this young girl betrayed by her protector. It was after her burial——"

"Cease!" cried a voice, smooth, fresh, and yet strangely commanding, from over Thomas's shoulder. "Let me tell the rest. No man can tell the rest as I can."

"Felix!" ejaculated Amos Cadwalader below his breath.

"Felix!" repeated Thomas, shaken to his very heart by this new presence. But when he sought to rise, to turn, he felt the pressure of a hand on his shoulder and heard that voice again, saying softly, but peremptorily:

"Wait! Wait till you hear what I have to say. Think not of me, think only of her. It is she you are called upon to avenge; your sister, Evelyn."

Thomas yielded to him as he had to his father. He sank down beneath that insistent hand, and his brother took up the tale.

"Evelyn had a voice like a bird. In those days before father's return, she used to fill old John Poindexter's house with melody. I, who, as a boy, was studious, rather than artistic, thought she sang too much for a girl whose father was rotting away in a Southern prison. But when about to rebuke her, I remembered Edward Kissam, and was silent. For it was his love which made her glad, and to him I wished every happiness, for he was good, and honest, and kind to me. She was eighteen then, and beautiful, or so I was bound to believe, since every man looked at her, even old John Poindexter, though he never looked at any other woman, not even his own wife. And she was good, too, and pure, I swear, for her blue eyes never faltered in looking into mine until one day when—my God! how well I remember it!—they not only faltered, but shrank before me in such terror, that, boy though I was, I knew that something terrible, something unprecedented had happened, and thinking my one thought, I asked if she had received bad news from father. Her answer was a horrified moan, but it might have been a shriek. 'Our father! Pray God we may never see him or hear from him again. If you love him, if you love me, pray he may die in prison rather than return here to see me as I am now.'

"I thought she had gone mad, and perhaps she had for a moment; for at my look of startled distress a change took place in her. She remembered my youth, and laughing, or trying to laugh away her frenzy, uttered some hurried words I failed to understand, and then, sinking at my knee, laid her head against my side, crying that she was not well; that she had experienced for a long time secret pains and great inward distress, and that she sometimes feared she was not going to live long, for all her songs and merry ways and seeming health and spirits.

"'Not live, Evelyn?' It was an inconceivable thought to me, a boy. I looked at her, and seeing how pale, how incomprehensibly pale she was, my heart failed me, for nothing but mortal sickness could make such a change in any one in a week, in a day. Yet how could death reach her, loved as she was by Edward, by her father, and by me. Thinking to rouse her, I spoke the former's name. But it was the last word I should have uttered. Crouching as if I had given her a blow, she put her two hands out, shrieking faintly: 'Not that! Never that! Do not speak his name. Let me never hear of him or see him again. I am dead—do you not understand me?—dead to all the world from this day—except to you!' she suddenly sobbed, 'except to you!' And still I did not comprehend her. But when I understood, as I soon did, that no mention was to be made of her illness; that her door was to be shut and no one allowed to enter, not even Mrs. Poindexter or her guardian—least of all, her guardian—I began to catch the first intimation of that horror which was to end my youth and fill my whole after life with but one thought—revenge. But I said nothing, only watched and waited. Seeing that she was really ill, I constituted myself her nurse, and sat by her night and day till her symptoms became so alarming that the whole household was aroused and we could no longer keep the doctor from her. Then I sat at her door, and with one ear turned to catch her lightest moan, listened for the step she most dreaded, but which, though it sometimes approached, never passed the opening of the hall leading to her chamber. For one whole week I sat there, watching her life go slowly out like a flame, with nothing to feed it; then as the great shadow fell, and life seemed breaking up within me, I dashed from the place, and confronting him where I found him walking, pale and disturbed, in his own hall, told him that my father was coming; that I had had a dream, and in that dream I had seen my father with his face turned toward this place. Was he prepared to meet him? Had he an answer ready when Amos Cadwalader should ask him what had become of his child?

"I had meant to shock the truth from this man, and I did so. As I mentioned my father's name, Poindexter blanched, and my fears became certainty. Dropping my youthful manner, for I was a boy no longer, I flung his crime in his face, and begged him to deny it if he could. He could not, but he did what neither he nor any other man could do in my presence now and live—he smiled. Then when he saw me crouching for a spring—for, young as I was, I knew but one impulse, and that was to fly at his throat—he put out his powerful hand, and pinning me to the ground, uttered a few short sentences in my ear.

"They were terrible ones. They made me see that nothing I might then do could obliterate the fact that she was lost if the world knew what I knew, or even so much as suspected it; that any betrayal on my part or act of contrition on his would only pile the earth on her innocent breast and sink her deeper and deeper into the grave she was then digging for herself; that all dreams were falsities; that Southern prisons seldom gave up their victims alive; and that if my father should escape the jaws of Libby and return, it was for me to be glad if he found a quiet grave instead of a dishonored daughter. Further, that if I crossed him, who was power itself, by any boyish exhibition of hate, I would find that any odium I might invoke would fall on her and not on him, making me an abhorrence, not only to the world at large, but to the very father in whose interest I might pretend to act.

"I was young and without worldly experience. I yielded to these arguments, but I cursed him where he stood. With his hand pressing heavily upon me, I cursed him to his face; then I went back to my sister.

"Had she, by some supernatural power, listened to our talk, or had she really been visited by some dream, that she looked so changed? There was a feverish light in her eye, and something like the shadow of a smile on her lips. Mrs. Poindexter was with her; Mrs. Poindexter, whose face was a mask we never tried to penetrate. But when she had left us alone again, then Evelyn spoke, and I saw what her dream had been.

"'Felix,' she cried as I approached her trembling with my own emotions and half afraid of hers, 'there is still one hope for me. It has come to me while you have been away. Edward—he loves me—did—perhaps he would forgive. If he would take me into his protection (I see you know it all, Felix) then I might grow happy again—well—strong—good. Do you think—oh, you are a child, what do you know?—but—but before I turn my face forever to the wall try if he will see me—try, try—with your boy's wit—your clever schemes, to get him here unknown to—to—the one I fear, I hate—and then, then, if he bids me live, I will live, and if he bids me die, I will die; and all will be ended.'

"I was an ignorant boy. I knew men no more than I knew women, and yielding to her importunities, I promised to see Edward and plan for an interview without her guardian's knowledge. I was, as Evelyn had said, keen in those days and full of resources, and I easily managed it. Edward, who had watched from the garden as I had from the door, was easily persuaded to climb her lattice in search of what he had every reason to believe would be his last earthly interview with his darling. As his eager form bounded into the room I tottered forth, carrying with me a vision of her face as she rose to meet—what? I dared not think or attempt to foresee. Falling on my knees I waited the issue. Alas! It was a speedy one. A stifled moan from her, the sound of a hoarse farewell from him, told me that his love had failed her, and that her doom was sealed. Creeping back to her side as quickly as my failing courage admitted, I found her face turned to the wall, from which it never again looked back; while presently, before the hour was passed, shouts ringing through the town proclaimed that young Kissam had shot himself. She heard, and died that night. In her last hour she had fancies. She thought she saw her father, and her prayers for mercy were heart-rending. Then she thought she saw him, that demon, her executioner, and cringed and moaned against the wall.

"But enough of this. Two days after, I walked between him and her silent figure outstretched for burial. I had promised that no eye but mine should look upon her, no other hand touch her, and I kept my word, even when the impossible happened and her father rose up in the street before us. Quietly, and in honor, she was carried to her grave, and then—then, in the solitude of the retreat I had found for him, I told our father all, and why I had denied him the only comfort which seemed left to him—a last look at his darling daughter's face."

CHAPTER II

THE OATH

A sigh from the panting breast of Amos Cadwalader followed these words. Plainer than speech it told of a grief still fresh and an agony still unappeased, though thirty years had passed away since the unhappy hour of which Felix spoke.

Felix, echoing it, went quickly on:

"It was dusk when I told my story, and from dark to dawn we sat with eyes fixed on each other's face, without sleep and without rest. Then we sought John Poindexter.

"Had he shunned us we might have had mercy, but he met us openly, quietly, and with all the indifference of one who cannot measure feeling, because he is incapable of experiencing it himself. His first sentence evinced this. 'Spare yourselves, spare me all useless recriminations. The girl is dead; I cannot call her back again. Enjoy your life, your eating and your drinking, your getting and your spending; it is but for a few more years at best. Why harp on old 'griefs?' His last word was a triumph. 'When a man cares for nothing or nobody, it is useless to curse him.'

"Ah, that was it! That was the secret of his power. He cared for nothing and for no one, not even for himself. We felt the blow, and bent under it. But before leaving him and the town, we swore, your father and I, that we would yet make that cold heart feel; that some day, in some way, we would cause that impassive nature to suffer as he had made us suffer, however happy he might seem or however closely his prosperity might cling to him. That was thirty years ago, and that oath has not yet been fulfilled."

Felix paused. Thomas lifted his head, but the old man would not let him speak. "There are men who forget in a month, others who forget in a year. I have never forgotten, nor has Felix here. When you were born (I had married again, in the hope of renewed joy) I felt, I know not why, that Evelyn's avenger was come. And when, a year or so after this event, we heard that God had forgotten John Poindexter's sins, or, perhaps, remembered them, and that a child was given him also, after eighteen years of married life, I looked upon your bonny face and saw—or thought I saw—a possible means of bringing about the vengeance to which Felix and I had dedicated our lives.

"You grew; your ardent nature, generous temper, and facile mind promised an abundant manhood, and when your mother died, leaving me for a second time a widower, I no longer hesitated to devote you to the purpose for which you seemed born. Thomas, do you remember the beginning of that journey which finally led you far from me? How I bore you on my shoulder along a dusty road, till arrived within sight of his home, I raised you from among the tombs and, showing you those distant gables looming black against the twilight's gold, dedicated you to the destruction of whatever happiness might hereafter develop under his infant's smile? You do? I did not think you could forget; and now that the time has come for the promise of that hour to be fulfilled, I call on you again, Thomas. Avenge our griefs, avenge your sister. *Poindexter's girl has grown to womanhood.*"

At the suggestion conveyed in these words Thomas recoiled in horror. But the old man failed to read his emotion rightly. Clutching his arm, he proceeded passionately:

"Woo her! Win her! They do not know you. You will be Thomas Adams to them, not Thomas Cadwalader. Gather this budding flower into your bosom, and then—Oh, he must love his child! Through her we have our hand on his heart. Make her suffer— she's but a country girl, and you have lived in Paris—make her suffer, and if, in doing so, you cause him to blench, then believe I am looking upon you from the grave I go to, and be happy; for you will not have lived, nor will I have died, in vain."

He paused to catch his failing breath, but his indomitable will triumphed over death and held Thomas under a spell that confounded his instincts and made him the puppet of feelings which had accumulated their force to fill him, in one hour, with a hate which it had taken his father and brother a quarter of a century to bring to the point of active vengeance.

"I shall die; I am dying now," the old man panted on. "I shall never live to see your triumph; I shall never behold John Poindexter's eye glaze with those sufferings which rend the entrails and make a man question if there is a God in heaven. But I shall know it where I am. No mounded earth can keep my spirit down when John Poindexter feels his doom. I shall be conscious of his anguish and shall rejoice; and when in the depths of darkness to which I go he comes faltering along my way——

"Boy, boy, you have been reared for this. God made you handsome; man has made you strong; you have made yourself intelligent and accomplished. You have only to show yourself to this country girl to become the master of her will and affection, and these once yours, remember *me*! *Remember Evelyn!*"

Never had Thomas been witness to such passion. It swept him along in a burning stream against which he sought to contend and could not. Raising his hand in what he meant as a response to that appeal, he endeavored to speak, but failed. His father misinterpreted his silence, and bitterly cried:

"You are dumb! You do not like the task; are virtuous, perhaps— you who have lived for years alone and unhampered in Paris. Or you have instincts of honor, habits of generosity that blind you to wrongs that for a longer space than your lifetime have cried aloud to heaven for vengeance. Thomas, Thomas, if you should fail me now——"

"He will not fail you," broke in the voice of Felix, calm, suave, and insinuating. "I have watched him; I know him; he will not fail you."

Thomas shuddered; he had forgotten Felix, but as he heard these words he could no longer delay looking at the man who had offered to stand his surety for the performance of the unholy deed his father exacted from him. Turning, he saw a man who in any place and under any roof would attract attention, awake admiration and—yes, fear. He was not a large man, not so large as himself, but the will that expressed itself in frenzy on his father's lips showed quiet and inflexible in the gray eye resting upon his own with a power he could never hope to evade. As he looked and comprehended, a steel band seemed to compress his heart; yet he was conscious at the same time that the personality before which he thus succumbed was as elegant as his own and as perfectly trained in all the ways of men and of life. Even the air of poverty which had shocked him in his father's person and surroundings was not visible here. Felix was both well and handsomely clad, and could hold his own as the elder brother in every respect most insisted upon by the Parisian gentleman. The long and, to Thomas, mysterious curtain of dark-green serge which stretched behind him from floor to ceiling threw out his pale features with a remarkable distinctness, and for an instant Thomas wondered if it had been hung there for the purpose of producing this effect. But the demand in his brother's face drew his attention, and, bowing his head, he stammered:

"I am at your command, Felix. I am at your command, father. I cannot say more. Only remember that I never saw Evelyn, that she died before I was born, and that I——"

But here Felix's voice broke in, kind, but measured:

"Perhaps there is some obstacle we have not reckoned upon. You may already love some woman and desire to marry her. If so, it need be no impediment——"

But here Thomas's indignation found voice.

"No," said he; "I am heart-whole save for a few lingering fancies which are fast becoming vanishing dreams."

He seemed to have lived years since entering this room.

"Your heart will not be disturbed now," commented Felix. "I have seen the girl. I went there on purpose a year ago. She's as pale as a snow-drop and as listless. You will not be obliged to recall to mind the gay smiles of Parisian ladies to be proof against her charms."

Thomas shrugged his shoulders.

"She must be made to know the full intoxication of hope," Felix proceeded in his clear and cutting voice. "To realize despair she must first experience every delight that comes with satisfied love. Have you the skill as well as heart to play to the end a rôle which will take patience as well as dissimulation, courage as well as subtlety, and that union of will and implacability which finds its food in tears and is strengthened, rather than lessened, by the suffering of its victim?"

"I have the skill," murmured Thomas, "but——"

"You lack the incentive," finished Felix. "Well, well, we must have patience with your doubts and hesitations. Our hate has been fostered by memories of her whom, as you say, you have never seen. Look, then, Thomas. Look at your sister as she was, as she is for us. Look at her, and think of her as despoiled, killed, forgotten by Poindexter. Have you ever gazed upon a more moving countenance, or one in which beauty contends with a keener prophecy of woe?"

Not knowing what to expect, anticipating almost to be met by her shade, Thomas followed the direction of his brother's lifted hand, and beheld, where but a minute before that dismal curtain had hung, a blaze of light, in the midst of which he saw a charming, but tragic, figure, such as no gallery in all Europe had ever shown him, possibly because no other limned face or form had ever appealed to his heart. It did not seem a picture, it seemed her very self, a gentle, loving self that breathed forth all the tenderness he had vainly sought for in his living relatives; and falling at her feet, he cried out:

"Do not look at me so reproachfully, sweet Evelyn. I was born to avenge you, and I will. John Poindexter shall never go down in peace to his tomb."

A sigh of utter contentment came from the direction of the bed.

"Swear it!" cried his father, holding out his arms before him in the form of a cross.

"Yes, swear it!" repeated Felix, laying his own hand on those crossed arms.

Thomas drew near, and laid his hand beside that of Felix.

"I swear," he began, raising his voice above the tempest, which poured gust after gust against the house. "I swear to win the affections of Eva Poindexter, and then, when her heart is all mine, to cast her back in anguish and contumely on the breast of John Poindexter."

"Good!" came from what seemed to him an immeasurable distance. Then the darkness, which since the taking of this oath had settled over his senses, fell, and he sank insensible at the feet of his dying father.

Amos Cadwalader died that night; but not without one awful scene more. About midnight he roused from the sleep which had followed the exciting incidents I have just related, and glancing from Thomas to Felix, sitting on either side of the bed, fixed his eyes with a strange gleam upon the door.

"Ah!" he ejaculated, "a visitor! John Poindexter! He comes to ask my forgiveness before I set out on my dismal journey."

The sarcasm of his tone, the courtesy of his manner, caused the hair to stir on the heads of his two sons. That he saw his enemy as plainly as he saw them, neither could doubt.

"Does he dread my meeting with Evelyn? Does he wish to placate me before I am joined to that pathetic shade? He shall not be disappointed. I forgive you, John Poindexter! I forgive you my daughter's shame, my blighted life. I am dying; but I leave one behind who will not forgive you. I have a son, an avenger of the dead, who yet lives to—to——"

He fell back. With these words, which seemed to seal Thomas to his task, Amos Cadwalader died.

CHAPTER III

EVA

Felix had not inherited his father's incapacity for making money. In the twenty years that had passed since Thomas had been abroad he had built up a fortune, which he could not induce his father to share, but which that father was perfectly willing to see devoted to their mutual revenge. There was meaning, therefore, in the injunction Felix gave his brother on his departure for Montgomery:

"I have money; spend it; spend what you will, and when your task is completed, there will still be some left for your amusement."

Thomas bowed. "The laborer is worthy of his hire," was his thought. "And you?" he asked, looking about the scanty walls, which seemed to have lost their very excuse for being now that his father had died. "Will you remain here?"

Felix's answer was abrupt, but positive. "No; I go to New York to-morrow. I have rented a house there, which you may one day wish to share. The name under which I have leased it is Adams, Felix Adams. As such you will address me. Cadwalader is a name that must not leave your lips in Montgomery, nor must you forget that my person is known there, otherwise we might not have been dependent on you for the success of our revenge." And he smiled, fully conscious of being the handsomer man of the two. "And now how about those introductions we enjoined you to bring from Paris?"

The history of the next few weeks can best be understood by reading certain letters sent by Thomas to Felix, by examining a diary drawn up by the same writer for his own relief and satisfaction. The letters will be found on the left, and the diary on the right, of the double columns hereby submitted. The former are a summary of facts; the latter is a summary of feelings. Both are necessary to a right comprehension of the situation.

FIRST LETTER.

DEAR FELIX:

I am here; I have seen her. She is, as you have said, a pale blonde. To-morrow I present my credentials to John Poindexter. From what I have already experienced I anticipate a favorable reception.

Yours aff., THOMAS.

FIRST ENTRY.

I could not write Felix the true story of this day. Why? And why must I write it here? To turn my mind from dwelling on it? Perhaps. I do not seem to understand my own feelings, or why I begin to dread my task, while ardently pressing forward to accomplish it.

I have seen her. This much I wrote to Felix, but I did not say where our meeting took place or how. How could I? Would he understand how one of Poindexter's blood could be employed in a gracious act, or how I, filled with a purpose that has made my heart dark as hell ever since I embraced it, could find that heart swell and that purpose sink at my first glimpse of the face whose beauty I have sworn to devote to agony and tears? Surely, surely Felix would have been stronger, and yet—

—

I went from the cars to the cemetery. Before entering the town or seeing to my own comfort, I sought Evelyn's grave, there to renew my oath in the place where, nineteen years ago, my father held me up, a four-year-old child, in threat, toward John

Poindexter's home. I had succeeded in finding the old and neglected stone which marked her resting-place, and was bending in the sunset light to examine it, when the rustle of a woman's skirts attracted my attention, and I perceived advancing toward me a young girl in a nimbus of rosy light which seemed to lift her from the ground and give to her delicate figure and strangely illumined head an ethereal aspect which her pure features and tender bearing did not belie. In her arms she carried a huge cluster of snow-white lilies, and when I observed that her eyes were directed not on me, but on the grave beside which I stood, I moved aside into the shadow of some bushes and watched her while she strewed these flowers— emblems of innocence—over the grave I had just left.

What did it mean, and who was this young girl who honored with such gracious memorials the grave of my long-buried sister? As she rose from her task I could no longer restrain either my emotion or the curiosity with which her act had inspired me. Advancing, I greeted her with all the respect her appearance called for, and noting that her face was even more beautiful when lifted in speech than when bent in gravity over her flowers, I asked her, in the indifferent tone of a stranger, who was buried in this spot, and why she, a mere girl, dropped flowers upon a grave the mosses of whose stone proved it to have been dug long before she was born.

Her answer caused me a shock, full as my life has lately been of startling experiences. "I strew flowers here," said she, "because the girl who lies buried under this stone had the same birthday as myself. I never saw her, it's true, but she died in my father's house when she was no older than I am to-day, and since I have become a woman and realize what loss there is in dying young, I have made it a custom to share with her my birthday flowers. She was a lily, they say, in appearance and character, and so I bring her lilies."

It was Eva Poindexter, the girl I—And she was strewing flowers on Evelyn's grave.

LETTER II.

ENTRY II.

DEAR FELIX:

I have touched the hand of John

I no longer feel myself a true man. John Poindexter is cold in appearance, hard in manner,

Poindexter. In order to win a place in the good graces of the daughter I must please the father, or at least attract his favorable notice. I have reason to think I have done this.

Very truly, THOMAS.

and inflexible in opinion, but he does not inspire the abhorrence I anticipated nor awaken in me the one thought due to the memory of my sister. Is it because he is Eva's father? Has the loveliness of the daughter cast a halo about the parent? If so, Felix has a right to execrate me and my father to——

LETTER III.

ENTRY III.

DEAR FELIX:

The introductions furnished me have made me received everywhere. There is considerable wealth here and many fine houses. Consequently I find myself in a congenial society, of which she is the star. Did I say that he was, as of old, the chief man of the town?

Yours truly, THOMAS.

She is beautiful. She has the daintiness of the lily and the flush of the rose. But it is not her beauty that moves me; it is the strange sweetness of her nature, which, nevertheless, has no weakness in it; on the contrary, it possesses peculiar strength, which becomes instantly apparent at the call of duty. Could Felix have imagined such a Poindexter? I cannot contemplate such loveliness and associate it with the execrable sin which calls down vengeance upon this house. I cannot even dwell upon my past life. All that is dark, threatening, secret, and revengeful slips from me under her eye, and I dream of what is pure, true, satisfying, and ennobling. And this by the influence of her smile, rather than of her words. Have I been given an angel to degrade? Or am I so blind as to behold a saint where others (Felix, let us say) would see only a pretty woman with unexpected attractions?

LETTER IV.	ENTRY IV.

DEAR FELIX:

Rides, dances, games, nonsense generally. My interest in this young girl is beginning to be publicly recognized. She alone seems ignorant of it. Sometimes I wonder if our scheme will fail through her impassibility and more than conventional innocence. I am sometimes afraid she will never love me. Yet I have exerted myself to please her. Indeed, I could not have exerted myself more. To-day I went twenty-five miles on horseback to procure her a trifle she fancied.

Yours aff., THOMAS.

All will not go as easily as Felix imagines. Eva Poindexter may be a country girl, but she has her standards, too, and mere grace and attainment are not sufficient to win her. Have I the other qualities she demands? That remains to be seen. I have one she never dreams of. Will its shadow so overwhelm the rest that her naturally pure spirit will shrink from me just at the moment when I think her mine? I cannot tell, and the doubt creates a hell within me. Something deeper, stronger, more imperious than my revenge makes the winning of this girl's heart a necessity to me. I have forgotten my purpose in this desire. I have forgotten everything except that she is the one woman of my life, and that I can never rest till her heart is wholly mine. Good

God! Have I become a slave where I hoped to be master? Have I, Thomas Cadwalader, given my soul into the keeping of this innocent girl? I do not even stop to inquire. To win her—that is all for which I now live.

LETTER V.

ENTRY V.

DEAR FELIX:

She may not care for me, but she is interested in no one else. Of this I am assured by John Poindexter, who seems very desirous of aiding me in my attempt to win his daughter's heart. Hard won, close bound. If she ever comes to love me it will be with the force of a very strong nature. The pale blonde has a heart.

Yours aff., THOMAS.

If it were passion only that I feel, I might have some hope of restraining it. But it is something more, something deeper, something which constrains me to look with her eyes, hear with her ears, and throb with her heart. My soul, rather than my senses, is enthralled. I want to win her, not for my own satisfaction, but to make her happy. I want to prove to her that goodness exists in this world—I, who came here to corrode and destroy; I, who am still pledged to do so. Ah, Felix, Felix, you should have chosen an older man for your purpose, or remembered that he who could be influenced as I was by family affections possesses a heart too soft for such infamy.

ENTRY VI.

The name of Evelyn is never mentioned in this house. Sometimes I think that he has forgotten her, and find in this thought the one remaining spur to my revenge. Forgotten her! Strange, that his child, born long after his victim's death, should remember this poor girl, and he forget! Yet on the daughter the blow is planned to fall—if it does fall. Should I not pray that it never may? That she should loathe instead of love me? Distrust, instead of confide in my honor and affection? But who can pray against himself? Eva Poindexter must love me, even if I am driven to self-destruction by my own remorse, after she has confided her heart to my keeping.

LETTER VI.

ENTRY VII.

DEAR FELIX:

Will you send me a few exquisite articles from Tiffany's? I see that her father expects me to give her presents. I think she will accept them. If she does, we may both

I cannot bring myself to pass a whole day away from her side. If Felix were here and could witness my assiduity, he would commend me in his cold and inflexible heart for the rest easy as to the state of her affections.

Very truly, THOMAS.

singleness with which I pursue my purpose. He would say to me, in the language of one of his letters: "You are not disappointing us." Us! As if our father still hovered near, sharing our purposes and hope. Alas! if he does, he must penetrate more deeply than Felix into the heart of this matter; must see that with every day's advantage—and I now think each day brings its advantage—I shrink further and further from the end they planned for me; the end which can alone justify my advance in her affections. I am a traitor to my oath, for I now know I shall never disappoint Eva's faith in me. I could not. Rather would I meet my father's accusing eyes on the verge of that strange world to which he has gone, or Felix's recriminations here, or my own contempt for the weakness which has made it possible for me to draw back from the brink of this wicked revenge to which I have devoted myself.

LETTER VII.

ENTRY VIII.

DEAR FELIX:

I hate John Poindexter, yes, I hate him, but I can never hate

This morning I passed under the window you have described to me as Evelyn's. I did it with a purpose. I wanted to test my own emotions and to see how much feeling it would arouse in me. Enough.

Eva accepted the brooch. It was the simplest thing you sent.

Aff., THOMAS.

his daughter. Only Felix could so confound the father with the child as to visit his anger upon this gentle embodiment of all that is gracious, all that is trustworthy, all that is fascinating in woman. But am I called upon to hate her? Am I not in a way required to love her? I will ask Felix. No, I cannot ask Felix. He would never comprehend her charm or its influence over me. He would have doubts and come at once to Montgomery. Good God! Am I proving such a traitor to my own flesh and blood that I cannot bear to think of Felix contemplating even in secret the unsuspicious form of his enemy's daughter?

LETTER VIII.

ENTRY IX.

DEAR FELIX:

A picnic on the mountains. It fell to me to escort Miss Poindexter down a dangerous slope. Though no words of affection passed between us (she is not yet ready for them), I feel that I have made a decided advance in her good graces.

Yours, THOMAS.

I have touched her hand! I have felt her sweet form thrilling against mine as we descended the mountain ledges together! No man was near, no eye— there were moments in which we were as much alone in the wide paradise of these wooded slopes as if the world held no other breathing soul. Yet I no more dared to press her hand, or pour forth the mad worship of my heart into her innocent ears, than if the eyes of all Paris had been upon us. How I love her! How far off and faint seem the years of that dead crime my brother would invoke for the punishment of this sweet soul! Yes, and how remote that awful hour in which I knelt beneath the hand of my dying father and swore—Ah, that oath! That oath!

ENTRY X.

The thing I dreaded, the thing I might have foreseen, has occurred. Felix has made his appearance in Montgomery. I received a communication to that effect from him to-day; a communication in which he commands me to meet him to-night, at Evelyn's grave, at the witching hour of twelve. I do not enjoy the summons. I have a dread of Felix, and begin to think he calculates upon stage devices to control me. But the day has passed for that. I will show him that I can be no more influenced in that place and at that hour than I could be in this hotel room, with the sight of her little glove—is there sin in such thefts?—lying on the table before us. Evelyn! She is a sacred memory. But the dead must not interfere with the living. Eva shall never be sacrificed to Evelyn's manes, not if John Poindexter lives out his life to his last hour in peace; not if Felix—well; I need to play the man; Felix is a formidable antagonist to meet, alone, in a spot of such rancorous memories, at an hour when spirits—if there be spirits—haunt the precincts of the tomb.

ENTRY XI.

I should not have known Felix had I met him in the street. How much of a stranger he appeared, then, in the faint moonlight which poured upon that shaded spot! His very voice seemed altered, and in his manner I remarked a hesitation I had not supposed him capable of showing under any circumstances. Nor were his words such as I expected. The questions I dreaded most he did not ask. The recriminations I looked for he did not utter. He only told me coldly that my courtship must be shortened; that the end for which we were both prepared must be hastened, and gave me two weeks in which to bring matters to a climax. Then he turned to Evelyn's grave, and bending down, tried to read her name on the mossy stone. He was so long in doing this that I leaned down beside him and laid my hand on his shoulder. He was trembling, and his body was as cold as the stone he threw himself against. Was it the memory of her whom that stone covered which had aroused this emotion? If so, it was but natural. To all appearance he has never in all his life loved any one as he did this unhappy sister; and struck with a respect for the grief which has outlived many a man's lifetime, I was shrinking back when he caught my hand, and with a convulsive strain, contrasting strongly with his tone, which was strangely measured, he cried, "Do not forget the end! Do not forget John Poindexter! his sin, his indifference to my father's grief; the accumulated sufferings of years which made Amos Cadwalader a hermit amongst men. I have seen the girl; she has changed—women do change at her age—and some men, I do not say you, but some men might think her beautiful. But beauty, if she has it, must not blind your eyes, which are fixed upon another goal. Overlook it; overlook her—you have done so, have you not? Pale beauties cannot move one who has sat at the feet of the most dazzling of Parisian women. Keep your eyes on John Poindexter, the debt he owes us, and the suffering we have promised him. That she is sweet, gentle, different from all we thought her, only makes the chances of reaching his heart the greater. The worthier she may be of affections not indigenous to that hard soul, the surer will be our grip upon his nature and the heavier his downfall."

The old spell was upon me. I could neither answer nor assert myself. Letting go my hand, he rose, and with his back to the village—I noticed he had not turned his face to it since coming to this spot—he said: "I shall return to New York to-morrow. In two weeks you will telegraph your readiness to take up your abode with me. I have a home that will satisfy you; and it will soon be all your own."

Here he gripped his heart; and, dark as it was, I detected a strange convulsion cross his features as he turned into the moonlight. But it was gone before we could descend.

"You may hear from me again," he remarked somewhat faintly

as he grasped my hand, and turned away in his own direction. I had not spoken a word during the whole interview.

LETTER IX.

ENTRY XII.

DEAR FELIX:

I do not hear from you. Are you well, or did your journey affect your health? I have no especial advance to report. John Poindexter seems greatly interested in my courtship. Sometimes he gives me very good advice. How does that strike you, Felix?

Aff., THOMAS.

I shall never understand Felix. He has not left the town, but is staying here in hiding, watching me, no doubt, to see if the signs of weakening he doubtless suspects in me have a significance deep enough to overthrow his planned revenge. I know this, because I have seen him more than once during the last week, when he thought himself completely invisible. I have caught sight of him in Mr. Poindexter's grounds when Eva and I stood talking together in the window. I even saw him once in church, in a dark corner, to be sure, but where he could keep his eye upon us, sitting together in Mr. Poindexter's pew. He seemed to me thin that day. The suspense he is under is wearing upon him. Is it my duty to cut it short by proclaiming my infidelity to my oath and my determination to marry the girl who has made me forget it?

LETTER X.   ENTRY XIII.

DEAR FELIX:

Miss Poindexter has told me
unreservedly that she cares for
me. Are you satisfied with me
now?

In haste, THOMAS.

She loves me. Oh, ecstasy of
life! Eva Poindexter loves me. I
forced it from her lips to-day.
With my arms around her and
her head on my shoulder, I
urged her to confession, and it
came. Now let Felix do what he
will! What is old John
Poindexter to me? Her father.
What are Amos Cadwalader's
hatred and the mortal wrong
that called so loudly for
revenge? Dead issues, long
buried sorrows, which God
may remember, but which men
are bound to forget. Life, life
with her! That is the future
toward which I look; that is the
only vengeance I will take, the
only vengeance Evelyn can
demand if she is the angel we
believe her. I will write to Felix
to-morrow.

ENTRY XIV.

I have not written Felix. I had not the courage.

ENTRY XV.

I have had a dream. I thought I saw the meeting of my father with the white shade of Evelyn in the unimaginable recesses of that world to which both have gone. Strange horrors, stranger glories met as their separate paths crossed, and when the two forms had greeted and parted, a line of light followed the footsteps of the one and a trail of gloom those of the other. As their ways divided, I heard my father cry:

"There is no spot on your garments, Evelyn. Can it be that the wrongs of earth are forgotten here? That mortals remember what the angels forget, and that our revenge is late for one so blessed?"

I did not hear the answer, for I woke; but the echo of those words has rung in my ears all day. "Is our revenge late for one so blessed?"

ENTRY XVI.

I have summoned up courage. Felix has been here again, and the truth has at last been spoken between us. I had been pressing Eva to name our wedding day, and we were all standing—that is, John Poindexter, my dear girl, and myself—in the glare of the drawing-room lights, when I heard a groan, too faint for other ears to catch, followed by a light fall from the window overlooking the garden. It was Felix. He had been watching us, had seen my love, heard me talk of marriage, and must now be in the grounds in open frenzy, or secret satisfaction, it was hard to tell which. Determined to know, determined to speak, I excused myself on some hurried plea, and searched the paths he knew as well as I. At last I came upon him. He was standing near an old dial, where he had more than once seen Eva and me together. He was very pale, deathly pale, it seemed to me, in the faint starlight shining upon that open place; but he greeted me as usual very quietly and with no surprise, almost, in fact, as if he knew I would recognize his presence and follow him.

"You are playing your rôle well," said he; "too well. What was that I heard about your marrying?"

The time had come. I was determined to meet it with a man's courage. But I found it hard. Felix is no easy man to cross, even in small things, and this thing is his life, nay, more—his past, present, and future existence.

I do not know who spoke first. There was some stammering, a few broken words; then I heard myself saying distinctly, and with a certain hard emphasis born of the restraint I put upon myself:

"I love her! I want to marry her. You must allow this. Then——
"

I could not proceed. I felt the shock he had received almost as if it had been communicated to me by contact. Something that was not of the earth seemed to pass between us, and I remember raising my hand as if to shield my face. And then, whether it was the blowing aside of some branches which kept the moonlight from us, or because my eyesight was made clearer by my emotion, I caught one glimpse of his face and became conscious of a great suffering, which at first seemed the wrenching of my own heart, but in another moment impressed itself upon me as that of his, Felix's.

I stood appalled.

My weakness had uprooted the one hope of his life, or so I thought; and that he expressed this by silence made my heart yearn toward him for the first time since I recognized him as my brother. I tried to stammer some excuse. I was glad when the darkness fell again, for the sight of his bowed head and set features was insupportable to me. It seemed to make it easier for me to talk; for me to dilate upon the purity, the goodness which had robbed me of my heart in spite of myself. My heart! It seemed a strange word to pass between us two in reference to a Poindexter, but it was the only one capable of expressing the feeling I had for this young girl. At last, driven to frenzy by his continued silence, which had something strangely moving in it, I cried:

"You have never loved a woman, Felix. You do not know what the passion is when it seizes upon a man jaded with the hollow pleasures of an irresponsible life. You cannot judge; therefore you cannot excuse. You are made of iron——"

"Hush!" It was the first word he

had spoken since I had opened my heart to him. "You do not know what you are saying, Thomas. Like all egotists, you think yourself alone in experience and suffering. Will you think so when I tell you that there was a time in my life when I did not sleep for weeks; when the earth, the air, yes, and the heavens were full of nothing but her name, her face, her voice? When to have held her in my arms, to have breathed into her ear one word of love, to have felt her cheek fall against mine in confidence, in passion, in hope, would have been to me the heaven which would have driven the devils from my soul forever? Thomas, will you believe I do not know the uttermost of all you are experiencing, when I here declare to you that there has been an hour in my life when, if I had felt she could have been brought to love me, I would have sacrificed Evelyn, my own soul, our father's hope, John Poindexter's punishment, and become the weak thing you are to-day, and gloried in it, I, Felix Cadwalader, the man of iron, who has never been known to falter? But, Thomas, I overcame that feeling. I crushed down that love, and I call upon you to do the same. You may marry her, but——"

What stopped him? His own

heart or my own impetuosity? Both, perhaps, for at that moment I fell at his feet, and seizing his hand, kissed it as I might a woman's. He seemed to grow cold and stiff under this embrace, which showed both the delirium I was laboring under and the relief I had gotten from his words. When he withdrew his hand, I feel that my doom was about to be spoken, and I was not wrong. It came in these words:

"Thomas, I have yielded to your importunity and granted you the satisfaction which under the same circumstances I would have denied myself. But it has not made me less hard toward you; indeed, the steel with which you say my heart is bound seems tightening about it, as if the momentary weakness in which I have indulged called for revenge. Thomas, go on your way; make the girl your wife—I had rather you would, since she is—what she is—but after she has taken your name, after she believes herself secure in her honorable position and your love, then you are to remember our compact and your oath—back upon John Poindexter's care she is to be thrown, shortly, curtly, without explanation or excuse; and if it costs you your life, you are to stand firm in this attitude, using but one weapon in the struggle which may open between you and her father, and that is, your name of Cadwalader. You will not need any other. Thomas, do you swear to this? Or must I direct my own power against Eva Poindexter, and, by telling her your motive in courting her, make her hate you forever?"

"I will swear," I cried, overpowered by the alternative with which he threatened me. "Give me the bliss of calling her mine, and I will follow your wishes in all that concerns us thereafter."

"You will?" There was a sinister tone in this ejaculation that gave a shock to my momentary complacency. But we are so made that an anticipated evil affects us less than an immediate one; and remembering that weeks must yet elapse, during which he or John Poindexter or even myself might die, I said nothing, and he went icily on:

"I give you two months, alone and untrammelled. Then you are to bring your bride to my house, there to hear my final decision. There is to be no departure from this course. I shall expect you, Thomas; you and her. You can say that you are going to make her acquainted with your brother."

"I will be there," I murmured, feeling a greater oppression than when I took the oath at my father's death-bed. "I will be there."

There was no answer. While I was repeating those four words, Felix vanished.

LETTER XI.

ENTRY XVII.

DEAR FELIX:

Have a fresh draft made. I need cigars, clothes, and—a wedding ring. But no, let me stop short there. We will be married without one, unless you force it upon us. Eva's color is blue.

Very truly, THOMAS.

To-day I wrote again to Felix. He is at home, must be, for I have neither seen nor felt his presence since that fateful night. What did I write? I don't remember. I seem to be living in a dream. Everything is confused about me but Eva's face, Eva's smile. They are blissfully clear. Sometimes I wish they were not. Were they confused amid these shadows, I might have stronger hope of keeping my word to Felix. Now, I shall never keep it. Eva once my wife, separation between us will become impossible. John Poindexter is ill.

LETTER XII.

ENTRY XVIII.

DEAR FELIX:

Congratulations: visits from my neighbors; all the éclat we could wish or a true lover hate. The ring you sent fits as if made for her. I am called in all directions by a thousand duties. I am on exhibition, and every one's curiosity must be satisfied.

In haste, THOMAS.

LETTER XIII.

DEAR FELIX:

Eva is not pleased with the arrangements which have been made for our wedding. John Poindexter likes show; she does not. Which will carry the day?

Yours aff., THOMAS.

LETTER XIV.

DEAR FELIX:

A compromise has been effected. The wedding will be a quiet one, but not celebrated here. As you cannot wish to

The wedding is postponed. John Poindexter is very ill. Pray God, Felix hears nothing of this. He would come here; he would confront his enemy on his bed of sickness. He would denounce him, and Eva would be lost to me.

ENTRY XIX.

Mr. Poindexter is better, but our plans will have to be altered. We now think we will be married quietly, possibly in New York.

ENTRY XX.

We have decided to be married in New York. Mr. Poindexter needs the change, and Eva and I are delighted at the prospect of a private wedding. Then we attend it, I will not mention the place or hour of my marriage, only say that on September 27th at 4 P. M. you may expect my wife and myself at your house.

Aff., THOMAS.

will be near Felix, but not to subject ourselves to his will. Oh, no!

ENTRY XXI.

Married! She is mine. And now to confront Felix with my determination to hold on to my happiness. How I love her, and how I pity him! John Poindexter's wickedness is forgotten, Evelyn but a fading memory. The whole world seems to hold but three persons—Eva, Felix, and myself. How will it end? We meet at his home to-morrow.

CHAPTER IV

FELIX

Meanwhile there was another secret struggle going on in the depth of a nature from which all sympathy was excluded both by the temperament of the person concerned and the circumstances surrounding him.

I can but hint at it. Some tragedies lie beyond the ken of man, and this one we can but gather from stray scraps of torn-up letters addressed to no one and betraying their authorship only through the writer's hand. They were found long after the mystery of Felix Cadwalader's death had been fully accounted for, tucked away under the flooring of Bartow's room. Where or how procured by him, who can tell?

"Madness!

"I have seen Eva Poindexter again, and heaven and hell have contended for me ever since. Eva! Eva! the girl I thought of only as our prey. The girl I have given to my brother. She is too lovely for him: she is too lovely for any man unless it be one who has never before thrilled to any woman's voice, or seen a face that could move his passions or awaken his affection. Is it love I feel? Can I, Felix, who have had but one thought, known but one enthusiasm, retain in this breast of iron a spot however secret, however small, which any woman, least of all his daughter, could reach? Never! I am the prey of frenzy or the butt of devils. Yet only the inhabitants of a more celestial sphere brighten around me when I think of those half-raised eyes, those delicately parted lips, so devoid of guile, that innocent bearing, and the divine tenderness, mingled with strength, by which she commands admiration and awakens love. I must fly. I must never see her again. Thomas's purpose is steady. He must never see that mine rocks like an idol smitten by a thunderbolt.

"If Thomas had not been reared in Paris, he too—But I am the only weak one. Curses on my——

"Did I say I would fly? I cannot, not yet. One more glimpse of her face, if only to satisfy myself that I have reason for this madness. Perhaps I was but startled yesterday to find a celestial loveliness where I expected to encounter pallid inanity. If my emotion is due to my own weakness rather than to her superiority, I had better recognize my folly before it proves my destruction.

I will stay and——

Thomas will not, shall not——

dexter's daughter——

hate, hate for Thom——

"My self-esteem is restored. I have seen her again—him—they were together—there was true love in his eye—how could I expect him not to love her—and I was able to hide my anguish and impose his duty on him. She loves him—or he thinks so—and the work goes on. But I will not stay to watch its accomplishment. No, no.

"I told him my story to-night, under the guise of a past experience. Oh, the devils must laugh at us men! They have reason to. Sometimes I wonder if my father in the clearness of his new vision does not join them in their mirth.

"Home with my unhappy secret! Home, where nothing comes to distract me from my gnawing griefs and almost intolerable thoughts. I walk the floors. I cry aloud her name. I cry it even under the portrait of Evelyn. There are moments when I am tempted to write to Thomas—to forbid him——

"Eva! Eva! Eva! Every fibre in my miserable body utters the one word. But no man shall ever know. Thomas shall never know how the thought of her fills my days and nights, making my life a torment and the future——

"I wait for his letters (scanty they are and cold) as the doomed criminal awaits his executioner. Does she really love him? Or will that exquisite, that soulful nature call for a stronger mate, a more concentrated temperament, a—a——

"I thought I saw in one of my dark hours my father rising up from his grave to curse me. Oh! he might curse on if——

"What have I said about no man knowing? Bartow knows. In his dumbness, his deafness, he has surprised my secret, and shows that he has done so by his peering looks, his dissatisfied ways, and a jealousy at which I could shout aloud in mirth, if I were not more tempted to shriek aloud in torment. A dumb serving-man, picked up I have almost forgotten where, jealous of my weakness for John Poindexter's daughter! He was never jealous of my feeling for Evelyn. Yet till the day I dared fate by seeking out and looking for the second time upon the woman whose charms I had scorned, her name often resounded through these rooms, and my eyes dwelt upon but one spot, and that was where her picture hangs in the woeful beauty which has become my reproach.

"I have had a great surprise. The starling, which has been taught to murmur Evelyn's name, to-day shrieked out, 'Eva! Eva!' My first impulse was to wring its neck, my next to take it from its cage and hide it in my bosom. But I did neither. I am still a man.

"Bartow will wring that bird's neck if I do not. This morning I caught him with his hand on the cage and a murderous light in his eye, which I had no difficulty in understanding. Yet he cannot hear the word the wretched starling murmurs. He only knows it is a word, a name, and he is determined to suppress it. Shall I string the cage up out of this old fellow's reach? His deafness, his inability to communicate with others, the exactness with which he obeys my commands as given him by my colored slides, his attention to my every wish, consequent upon his almost animal love for my person, are necessary to me now, while the bird—Ah! there it goes again, 'Eva! Eva!'

"Is it hate or love I feel, abhorrence or passion? Love would seek to save, but I have no thought of saving her, since she has acknowledged her love for Thomas, and since he—Oh, it is not now for Evelyn's sake I plan revenge, but for my own! These nights and days of torture—the revelation I have had of my own nature—the consent I was forced to give to a marriage which means bliss to them and anguish beyond measure to me—all this calls for vengeance, and they will not escape, these two. I have laid my plans deep. I have provided for every contingency. It has taken time, thought, money. But the result is good. If they cross the threshold of my circular study, they must consent to my will or perish here, and I with them. Oh, they shall never live and be happy! Thomas need not think it. John Poindexter need not think it! I might have forgotten the oath made on my father's crossed arms, but I will never forget the immeasurable griefs of these past months or the humiliation they have brought me. My own weakness is to be avenged—my unheard-of, my intolerable weakness. Remember Evelyn? Remember Felix! Ah, again! Eva! Eva! Eva!"

CHAPTER V

WHY THE IRON SLIDE REMAINED
STATIONARY

The rest must be told in Thomas's own words, as it forms the chief part of the confession he made before the detectives:

According to my promise, I took my young wife to Felix's house on the day and at the hour proposed. We went on foot, for it was not far from the hotel where we were then staying, and were received at the door by an old servant who I had been warned could neither speak nor hear. At sight of him and the dim, old-fashioned hall stretching out in aristocratic gloom before us, Eva turned pale and cast me an inquiring look. But I reassured her with a smile that most certainly contradicted my own secret dread of the interview before us, and taking her on my arm, followed the old man down the hall, past the open drawing-room door (where I certainly thought we should pause), into a room whose plain appearance made me frown, till Bartow, as I have since heard him called, threw aside the portière at one end and introduced us into my brother's study, which at that moment looked like fairyland, or would have, if Felix, who was its sole occupant, had not immediately drawn our attention to himself by the remarkable force of his personality, never so impressive as at that moment.

Eva, to whom I had said little of this brother, certainly nothing which would lead her to anticipate seeing either so handsome a man or one of such mental poise and imposing character, looked frightened and a trifle awe-struck. But she advanced quite bravely toward him, and at my introduction smiled with such an inviting grace that I secretly expected to see him more or less disarmed by it.

And perhaps he was, for his already pale features turned waxy in the yellow glare cast by the odd lantern over our heads, and the hand he had raised in mechanical greeting fell heavily, and he could barely stammer out some words of welcome. These would have seemed quite inadequate to the occasion if his eyes which were fixed on her face, had not betrayed the fact that he was not without feeling, though she little realized the nature of that feeling or how her very life (for happiness is life) was trembling in the balance under that indomitable will.

I who did know—or thought I did—cast him an imploring glance, and, saying that I had some explanations to make, asked if Mrs. Adams might not rest here while we had a few words apart.

He answered me with a strange look. Did he feel the revolt in my tone and understand then as well as afterward what the nature of my compliance had been? I shall never know. I only know that he stopped fumbling with some small object on the table before him, and, bowing with a sarcastic grace that made me for the first time in my intercourse with him feel myself his inferior, even in size, led the way to a small door I had failed to notice up to this moment.

"Your wife will find it more comfortable here," he observed, with slow pauses in his speech that showed great, but repressed, excitement. And he opened the door into what had the appearance of a small but elegant sleeping-apartment. "What we have to say cannot take long. Mrs. Adams will not find the wait tedious."

"No," she smiled, with a natural laugh, born, as I dare hope, of her perfect happiness. Yet she could not but have considered the proceeding strange, and my manner, as well as his, scarcely what might be expected from a bridegroom introducing his bride to his only relative.

"I will call you—" I began, but the vision of her dimpled face above the great cluster of roses she carried made me forget to complete my sentence, and the door closed, and I found myself face to face with Felix.

He was breathing easier, and his manner seemed more natural now that we were alone, yet he did not speak, but cast a strange, if not inquiring, glance about the room (the weirdest of apartments, as you all well know), and seeming satisfied with what he saw, why I could not tell, led the way up to the large table which from the first had appeared to exert a sort of uncanny magnetism upon him, saying:

"Come further away. I need air, breathing place in this close room, and so must you. Besides, why should she hear what we have to say? She will know the worst soon enough. She seems a gentle-hearted woman."

"An angel!" I began, but he stopped me with an imperious gesture.

"We will not discuss your wi—Mrs. Adams," he protested. "Where is John Poindexter?"

"At the hotel," I rejoined. "Or possibly he has returned home. I no longer take account of his existence. Felix, I shall never leave my wife. I had rather prove recreant to the oath I took before I realized the worth of the woman whose happiness I vowed to destroy. This is what I have come to tell you. Make it easy for me, Felix. You are a man who has loved and suffered. Let us bury the past; let us——"

Had I hoped I could move him? Perhaps some such child's notion had influenced me up to this moment. But as these words left my lips, nay, before I had stumbled through them, I perceived by the set look of his features, which were as if cast in bronze, that I might falter, but that he was firm as ever, firmer, it seemed to me, and less easy to be entreated.

Yet what of that? At the worst, what had I to fear? A struggle which might involve Eva in bitter unpleasantness and me in the loss of a fortune I had come to regard almost as my own. But these were petty considerations. Eva must know sooner or later my real name and the story of her father's guilt. Why not now? And if we must start life poor, it was yet life, while a separation from her——

Meanwhile Felix had spoken, and in language I was least prepared to hear.

"I anticipated this. From the moment you pleaded with me for the privilege of marrying her, I have looked forward to this outcome and provided against it. Weakness on the part of her bridegroom was to be expected; I have, therefore, steeled myself to meet the emergency; for your oath must be kept!"

Crushed by the tone in which these words were uttered, a tone that evinced power against which any ordinary struggle would end in failure, I cast my eyes about the room in imitation of what I had seen him do a few minutes before. There was nothing within sight calculated to awaken distrust, and yet a feeling of distrust (the first I had really felt) had come with the look he had thrown above and around the mosque-like interior of the room he called his study. Was it the calm confidence he showed, or the weirdness of finding myself amid Oriental splendors and under the influence of night effects in high day and within sound of the clanging street cars and all the accompanying bustle of every-day traffic? It is hard to say; but from this moment on I found myself affected by a vague affright, not on my own account, but on hers whose voice we could plainly hear humming a gay tune in the adjoining apartment. But I was resolved to suppress all betrayal of uneasiness. I even smiled, though I felt the eyes of Evelyn's pictured countenance upon me; Evelyn's, whose portrait I had never lost sight of from the moment of entering the room, though I had not given it a direct look and now stood with my back to it. Felix, who faced it, but who did not raise his eyes to it, waited a moment for my response, and finding that my words halted, said again:

"That oath must be kept!"

This time I found words with which to answer. "Impossible!" I burst out, flinging doubt, fear, hesitancy, everything I had hitherto trembled at to the winds. "It was in my nature to take it, worked upon as I was by family affection, the awfulness of our father's approaching death, and a thousand uncanny influences all carefully measured and prepared for this end. But it is not in my nature to keep it after four months of natural living in the companionship of a man thirty years removed from his guilt, and of his guileless and wholly innocent daughter. And you cannot drive me to it, Felix. No man can force another to abandon his own wife because of a wicked oath taken long before he knew her. If you think your money——"

"Money?" he cried, with a contempt that did justice to my disinterestedness as well as his own. "I had forgotten I had it. No, Thomas, I should never weigh money against the happiness of living with such a woman as your wife appears to be. But her life I might. Carry out your threat; forget to pay John Poindexter the debt we owe him, and the matter will assume a seriousness for which you are doubtless poorly prepared. A daughter dead in her honeymoon will be almost as great a grief to him as a dishonored one. And either dead or dishonored he must find her, when he comes here in search of the child he cannot long forget. Which shall it be? Speak!"

Was I dreaming? Was this Felix? Was this myself? And was it in my ears these words were poured?

With a spring I reached his side where he stood close against the table, and groaned rather than shrieked the words:

"You would not kill her! You do not meditate a crime of blood—here—on her—the innocent—the good——"

"No," he said; "it will be you who will do that. You who will not wish to see her languish—suffer—go mad—Thomas, I am not the raving being you take me for. I am merely a keeper of oaths. Nay, I am more. I have talents, skill. The house in which you find yourself is proof of this. This room—see, it has no outlet save those windows, scarcely if at all perceptible to you, above our heads, and that opening shielded now by a simple curtain, but which in an instant, without my moving from this place, I can so hermetically seal that no man, save he be armed with crowbar and pickaxe, could enter here, even if man could know of our imprisonment, in a house soon to be closed from top to bottom by my departing servant."

"May God protect us!" fell from my lips, as, stiff with horror, I let my eyes travel from his determined face, first to the windows high over my head and then to the opening of the door, which, though but a few steps from where I stood, was as far as possible from the room into which my darling had been induced to enter.

Felix, watching me, uttered his explanations as calmly as if the matter were one of every-day significance. "You are looking for the windows," he remarked. "They are behind those goblin faces you see outlined on the tapestries under the ceiling. As for the door, if you had looked to the left when you entered, you would have detected the edge of a huge steel plate hanging flush with the casing. This plate can be made to slide across that opening in an instant just by the touch of my hand on this button. This done, no power save such as I have mentioned can move it back again, not even my own. I have forces at my command for sending it forward, but none for returning it to its place. Do you doubt my mechanical skill or the perfection of the electrical apparatus I have caused to be placed here? You need not, Thomas; nor need you doubt the will that has only to exert itself for an instant to—Shall I press the button, brother?"

"No, no!" I shouted in a frenzy, caused rather by my knowledge of the nature of this man than any especial threat apparent in his voice or gesture. "Let me think; let me know more fully what your requirements are—what she must suffer if I consent—and what I."

He let his hand slip back, that smooth white hand which I had more than once surveyed in admiration. Then he smiled.

"I knew you would not be foolish," he said. "Life has its charms even for hermits like me; and for a *beau garçon* such as you are——"

"Hush!" I interposed, maddened into daring his full anger. "It is not my life I am buying, but hers, possibly yours; for it seems you have planned to perish with us. Is it not so?"

"Certainly," was his cold reply. "Am I an assassin? Would you expect me to live, knowing you to be perishing?"

I stared aghast. Such resolve, such sacrifice of self to an idea was beyond my comprehension.

"Why—what?" I stammered. "Why kill us, why kill yourself——"

The answer overwhelmed me.

"Remember Evelyn!" shrilled a voice, and I paused, struck dumb with a superstitious horror I had never believed myself capable of experiencing. For it was not Felix who spoke, neither was it any utterance of my own aroused conscience. Muffled, strange, and startling it came from above, from the hollow spaces of that high vault lit with the golden glow that henceforth can have but one meaning for me—death.

"What is it?" I asked. "Another of your mechanical contrivances?"

He smiled; I had rather he had frowned.

"Not exactly. A favorite bird, a starling. Alas! he but repeats what he has heard echoed through the solitude of these rooms. I thought I had smothered him up sufficiently to insure his silence during this interview. But he is a self-willed bird, and seems disposed to defy the wrappings I have bound around him; which fact warns me to be speedy and hasten our explanations. Thomas, this is what I require: John Poindexter—you do not know where he is at this hour, but I do—received a telegram but now, which, if he is a man at all, will bring him to this house in a half-hour or so from the present moment. It was sent in your name, and in it you informed him that matters had arisen which demanded his immediate attention; that you were on your way to your brother's (giving him this address), where, if you found entrance, you would await his presence in a room called the study; but that—and here you will see how his coming will not aid us if that steel plate is once started on its course—if the possible should occur and your brother should be absent from home, then he was to await a message from you at the Plaza. The appearance of the house would inform him whether he would find you and Eva within; or so I telegraphed him in your name.

"Thomas, if Bartow fulfils my instructions—and I have never know him to fail me—he will pass down these stairs and out of this house in just five minutes. As he is bound on a long-promised journey, and as he expects me to leave the house immediately after him, he has drawn every shade and fastened every lock. Consequently, on his exit, the house will become a tomb, to which, just two weeks from to-day, John Poindexter will be called again, and in words which will lead to a demolition which will disclose—what? Let us not forestall the future, our horrible future, by inquiring. But Thomas, shall Bartow go? Shall I not by signs he comprehends more readily than other men comprehend speech indicate to him on his downward passage to the street that I wish him to wait and open the door to the man whom we have promised to overwhelm in his hour of satisfaction and pride? You have only to write a line—see! I have made a copy of the words you must use, lest your self-command should be too severely taxed. These words left on this table for his inspection—for you must go and Eva remain—will tell him all he needs to know from you. The rest can come from my lips after he has read the signature, which in itself will confound him and prepare the way for what I have to add. Have you anything to say against this plan? Anything, I mean, beyond what you have hitherto urged? Anything that I will consider or which will prevent my finger from pressing the button on which it rests?"

I took up the paper. It was lying on the table, where it had evidently been inscribed simultaneously with or just before our entrance into the house, and slowly read the few lines I saw written upon it. You know them, but they will acquire a new significance from your present understanding of their purpose and intent:

I return you back your daughter. Neither she nor you will ever see me again. Remember Evelyn!

AMOS'S SON.

"You wish me to sign these words, to put them into my own handwriting, and so to make them mine? Mine!" I repeated.

"Yes, and to leave them here on this table for him to see when he enters. He might not believe any mere statement from me in regard to your intentions."

I was filled with horror. Love, life, human hopes, the world's friendships—all the possibilities of existence, swept in one concentrated flood of thought and feeling through my outraged consciousness, and I knew I could never put my name to such a blasphemy of all that was sacred to man's soul. Tossing the paper in his face, I cried:

"You have gone too far! Better her death, better mine, better the destruction of us all, than such dishonor to the purest thing heaven ever made. I refuse, Felix—I refuse. And may God have mercy on us all!"

The moment was ghastly. I saw his face change, his finger tremble where it hovered above the fatal button; saw—though only in imagination as yet—the steely edge of that deadly plate of steel advancing beyond the lintel, and was about to dare all in a sudden grapple with this man, when a sound from another direction caught my ear, and looking around in terror of the only intrusion we could fear, beheld Eva advancing from the room in which we had placed her.

That moment a blood-red glow took the place of the sickly yellow which had hitherto filled every recess of this weird apartment. But I scarcely noticed the change, save as it affected her pallor and gave to her cheeks the color that was lacking in the roses at her belt.

Fearless and sweet as in the hour when she first told me that she loved me, she approached and stood before us.

"What is this?" she cried. "I have heard words that sound more like the utterances of some horrid dream than the talk of men and brothers. What does it mean, Thomas? What does it mean, Mr. — —"

"Cadwalader," announced Felix, dropping his eyes from her face, but changing not a whit his features or posture.

"Cadwalader?" The name was not to her what it was to her father. "Cadwalader? I have heard that name in my father's house; it was Evelyn's name, the Evelyn who——"

"Whom you see painted there over your head," finished Felix, "my sister, Thomas's sister—the girl whom your father—but I spare you, child though you be of a man who spared nothing. From your husband you may learn why a Cadwalader can never find his happiness with a Poindexter. Why thirty or more years after that young girl's death, you who were not then born are given at this hour the choice between death and dishonor. I allow you just five minutes in which to listen. After that you will let me know your joint decision. Only you must make your talk where you stand. A step taken by either of you to right or left, and Thomas knows what will follow."

Five minutes, with such a justification to make, and such a decision to arrive at! I felt my head swim, my tongue refuse its office, and stood dumb and helpless before her till the sight of her dear eyes raised in speechless trust to mine flooded me with a sense of triumph amid all the ghastly terrors of the moment, and I broke out in a tumult of speech, in excuses, explanations, all that comes to one in a more than mortal crisis.

She listened, catching my meaning rather from my looks than my words. Then as the minutes fled and my brother raised a warning hand, she turned toward him, and said:

"You are in earnest? We must separate in shame or perish in this prison-house with you?"

His answer was mere repetition, mechanical, but firm:

"You have said it. You have but one minute more, madam."

She shrank, and all her powers seemed leaving her, then a reaction came, and a flaming angel stood where but a moment before the most delicate of women weakly faltered; and giving me a look to see if I had the courage or the will to lift my hand against my own flesh and blood (alas for us both! I did not understand her) caught up an old Turkish dagger lying only too ready to her hand, and plunged it with one sideways thrust into his side, crying:

"We cannot part, we cannot die, we are too young, too happy!"

It was sudden; the birth of purpose in her so unexpected and so rapid that Felix, the ready, who was prepared for all contingencies, for the least movement or suggestion of escape, faltered and pressed, not the fatal button, but his heart.

One impulsive act on the part of a woman had overthrown all the fine-spun plans of the subtlest spirit that ever attempted to work its will in the face of God and man.

But I did not think of this then; I did not even bestow a thought upon the narrowness of our escape, or the price which the darling of my heart might be called upon to pay for this supreme act of self-defence. My mind, my heart, my interest were with Felix, in whom the nearness of death had called up all that was strongest and most commanding in his strong and commanding spirit.

Though struck to the heart, he had not fallen. It was as if the will which had sustained him through thirty years of mental torture held him erect still, that he might give her, Eva, one look, the like of which I had never seen on mortal face, and which will never leave my heart or hers until we die. Then as he saw her sink shudderingly down and the delicate woman reappear in her pallid and shrunken figure, he turned his eyes on me and I saw,—good God!—a tear well up from those orbs of stone and fall slowly down his cheek, fast growing hollow under the stroke of death.

"Eva! Eva! I love Eva!" shrilled the voice which once before had startled me from the hollow vault above.

Felix heard, and a smile faint as the failing rush of blood through his veins moved his lips and brought a revelation to my soul. He, too, loved Eva!

When he saw I knew, the will which had kept him on his feet gave way, and he sank to the floor murmuring:

"Take her away! I forgive. Save! Save! She did not know I loved her."

Eva, aghast, staring with set eyes at her work, had not moved from her crouching posture. But when she saw that speaking head fall back, the fine limbs settle into the repose of death, a shock went through her which I thought would never leave her reason unimpaired.

"I've killed him!" she murmured. "I've killed him!" and looking wildly about, her eyes fell on the cross that hung behind us on the wall. It seemed to remind her that Felix was a Catholic. "Bring it!" she gasped. "Let him feel it on his breast. It may bring him peace—hope."

As I rushed to do her bidding, she fell in a heap on the floor.

"Save!" came again from the lips we thought closed forever in death. And realizing at the words both her danger and the necessity of her not opening her eyes again upon this scene, I laid the cross in his arms, and catching her up from the floor, ran with her out of the house. But no sooner had I caught sight of the busy street and the stream of humanity passing before us, than I awoke to an instant recognition of our peril. Setting my wife down, I commanded life back into her limbs by the force of my own energy, and then dragging her down the steps, mingled with the crowd, encouraging her, breathing for her, living in her till I got her into a carriage and we drove away.

For the silence we have maintained from that time to this you must not blame Mrs. Adams. When she came to herself—which was not for days—she manifested the greatest desire to proclaim her act and assume its responsibility. But I would not have it. I loved her too dearly to see her name bandied about in the papers; and when her father was taken into our confidence, he was equally peremptory in enjoining silence, and shared with me the watch I now felt bound to keep over her movements.

But alas! His was the peremptoriness of pride rather than love. John Poindexter has no more heart for his daughter than he had for his wife or that long-forgotten child from whose grave this tragedy has sprung. Had Felix triumphed he would never have wrung the heart of this man. As he once said, when a man cares for nothing and nobody, not even for himself, it is useless to curse him.

As for Felix himself, judge him not, when you realize, as you now must, that his last conscious act was to reach for and put in his mouth the paper which connected Eva with his death. At the moment of death his thought was to save, not to avenge. And this after her hand had struck him.

CHAPTER VI

ANSWERED

A silence more or less surcharged with emotion followed this final appeal. Then, while the various auditors of this remarkable history whispered together and Thomas Adams turned in love and anxiety toward his wife, the inspector handed back to Mr. Gryce the memorandum he had received from him.

It presented the following appearance:

┌───┐
: Answered   :
└───┘

1. Why a woman who was calm enough to stop and arrange her hair during the beginning of an interview should be wrought up to such a pitch of frenzy and exasperation before it was over as to kill with her own hand a man she had evidently had no previous grudge against. (Remember the comb found on the floor of Mr. Adams's bedroom.)

┌───┐
: Answered   :
└───┘

2. What was the meaning of the following words, written just previous to this interview by the man thus killed: "I return you your daughter. Neither you nor she will ever see me again. Remember Evelyn!"

┌───┐
: Answered   :
└───┘

3. Why was the pronoun "I" used in this communication? What position did Mr. Felix Adams hold toward this young girl qualifying him to make use of such language after her marriage to his brother?

: Answered   :
---

4. And having used it, why did he, upon being attacked by her, attempt to swallow the paper upon which he had written these words, actually dying with it clinched between his teeth?

: Answered   :
---

5. If he was killed in anger and died as monsters do (her own word), why did his face show sorrow rather than hate, and a determination as far as possible removed from the rush of over-whelming emotions likely to follow the reception of a mortal blow from the hand of an unexpected antagonist?

: Answered   :
---

6. Why, if he had strength to seize the above-mentioned paper and convey it to his lips, did he not use that strength in turning on a light calculated to bring him assistance, instead of leaving blazing the crimson glow which, according to the code of signals as now understood by us, means: "Nothing more required just now. Keep away?"

: Answered   :
---

7. What was the meaning of the huge steel plate found between the casings of the doorway, and why did it remain at rest within its socket at this, the culminating, moment of his life?

: Answered   :
---

8. An explanation of how old Poindexter came to appear on the scene so soon after the event. His words as overheard were: "It is Amos' son, not Amos!" Did he not know whom he was to meet in this house? Was the condition of the man lying before him with a cross on his bosom and a dagger in his heart less of a surprise to him than the personality of the victim?

9. Remember the conclusions we have drawn from Bartow's pantomime. Mr. Adams was killed by a left-handed thrust. Watch for an acknowledgment that the young woman is left-handed, and do not forget that an explanation is due why for so long a time she held her other arm stretched out behind her.

10. Why did the bird whose chief cry is "Remember Evelyn!" sometimes vary it with "Poor Eva! Lovely Eva! Who would strike Eva?" The story of this tragedy, to be true, must show that Mr. Adams knew his brother's bride both long and well.

11. If Bartow is, as we think, innocent of all connection with this crime save as witness, why does he show such joy at its result? This may not reasonably be expected to fall within the scope of Thomas Adams's confession, but it should not be ignored by us. This deaf-and-dumb servitor was driven mad by the fact which caused him joy. Why?[2]

[2] It must be remembered that the scraps of writing in Felix's hand had not yet been found by the police. The allusions in them to Bartow show him to have been possessed by a jealousy which probably turned to delight when he saw his master smitten down by the object of that master's love and his own hatred. How he came to recognize in the bride of another man the owner of the name he so often saw hovering on the lips of his master, is a question to be answered by more astute students of the laws of perception than myself. Probably he spent much of his time at the loophole on the stairway, studying his master till he understood his every gesture and expression.

12. Notice the following schedule. It has been drawn up after repeated experiments with Bartow and the various slides of the strange lamp which cause so many different lights to shine out in Mr. Adams's study:

White light—Water wanted.Green light—Overcoat and hat to be brought.Blue light—Put back books on shelves.Violet light—Arrange study for the night.Yellow light—Watch for next light.Red light—Nothing wanted; stay away.

The last was on at the final scene. Note if this fact can be explained by Mr. Adams's account of the same.

Two paragraphs alone lacked complete explanation. The first, No. 9, was important. The description of the stroke dealt by Mr. Adams's wife did not account for this peculiar feature in Bartow's pantomime. Consulting with the inspector, Mr. Gryce finally approached Mr. Adams and inquired if he had strength to enact before them the blow as he had seen it dealt by his wife.

The startled young man looked the question he dared not ask. In common with others, he knew that Bartow had made some characteristic gestures in endeavoring to describe this crime, but he did not know what they were, as this especial bit of information had been carefully held back by the police. He, therefore, did not respond hastily to the suggestion made him, but thought intently for a moment before he thrust out his left hand and caught up some article or other from the inspector's table and made a lunge with it across his body into an imaginary victim at his right. Then he consulted the faces about him with inexpressible anxiety. He found little encouragement in their aspect.

"You would make your wife out left-handed," suggested Mr. Gryce. "Now I have been watching her ever since she came into this place, and I have seen no evidence of this."

"She is not left-handed, but she thrust with her left hand, because her right was fast held in mine. I had seized her instinctively as she bounded forward for the weapon, and the convulsive clutch of our two hands was not loosed till the horror of her act made her faint, and she fell away from me to the floor crying: 'Tear down the cross and lay it on your brother's breast. I would at least see him die the death of a Christian.'"

Mr. Gryce glanced at the inspector with an air of great relief. The mystery of the constrained attitude of the right hand which made Bartow's pantomime so remarkable was now naturally explained, and taking up the blue pencil which the inspector had laid down, he wrote, with a smile, a very decided "answered" across paragraph No. 9.

CHAPTER VII

LAST WORDS

A few minutes later Mr. Gryce was to be seen in the outer room, gazing curiously at the various persons there collected. He was seeking an answer to a question that was still disturbing his mind, and hoped to find it there. He was not disappointed. For in a quiet corner he encountered the amiable form of Miss Butterworth, calmly awaiting the result of an interference which she in all probability had been an active agent in bringing about.

He approached and smilingly accused her of this. But she disclaimed the fact with some heat.

"I was simply there," she explained. "When the crisis came, when this young creature learned that her husband had left suddenly for New York in the company of two men, then—why then, it became apparent to every one that a woman should be at her side who understood her case and the extremity in which she found herself. And I was that woman."

"You are always that woman," he gallantly replied, "if by the phrase you mean being in the right place at the right time. So you are already acquainted with Mrs. Adams's story?"

"Yes; the ravings of a moment told me she was the one who had handled the dagger that slew Mr. Adams. Afterward, she was able to explain the cause of what has seemed to us such a horrible crime. When I heard her story, Mr. Gryce, I no longer hesitated either as to her duty or mine. Do you think she will be called upon to answer for this blow? Will she be tried, convicted?"

"Madam, there are not twelve men in the city so devoid of intelligence as to apply the name of crime to an act which was so evidently one of self-defence. No true bill will be found against young Mrs. Adams. Rest easy."

The look of gloom disappeared from Miss Butterworth's eyes.

"Then I may return home in peace," she cried. "It has been a desperate five hours for me, and I feel well shaken up. Will you escort me to my carriage?"

Miss Butterworth did not look shaken up. Indeed, in Mr. Gryce's judgment, she had never appeared more serene or more comfortable. But she was certainly the best judge of her own condition; and after satisfying herself that the object of her care was reviving under the solicitous ministrations of her husband, she took the arm which Mr. Gryce held out to her and proceeded to her carriage.

As he assisted her in, he asked a few questions about Mr. Poindexter.

"Why is not Mrs. Adams's father here? Did he allow his daughter to leave him on such an errand as this without offering to accompany her?"

The answer was curtness itself:

"Mr. Poindexter is a man without heart. He came with us to New York, but refused to follow us to Police Headquarters. Sir, you will find that the united passions of three burning souls, and a revenge the most deeply cherished of any I ever knew or heard of, have been thrown away on a man who is positively unable to suffer. Do not mention old John Poindexter to me. And now, if you will be so good, tell the coachman to drive me to my home in Gramercy Park. I have put my finger in the police pie for the last time, Mr. Gryce—positively for the last time." And she sank back on the carriage cushions with an inexorable look, which, nevertheless, did not quite conceal a quiet complacency which argued that she was not altogether dissatisfied with herself or the result of her interference in matters usually considered at variance with a refined woman's natural instincts.

Mr. Gryce, in repressing a smile, bowed lower even than his wont, and, under the shadow of this bow, the carriage drove off. As he walked slowly back, he sighed. Was he wondering if a case of similar interest would ever bring them together again in consultation?

Lightning Source UK Ltd.
Milton Keynes UK
UKHW041822221118
332797UK00002B/410/P